Ans	_____	M.L.	_____
ASH	_____	MLW	_____
Bev	_____	Mt.Pl	_____
C.C.	_____	NLM	5/05 (June)
C.P.	_____	Ott	_____
Dick	_____	PC	_____
DRZ	_____	PH	_____
ECH	_____	P.P.	_____
ECS	_____	Pion.P.	5/07
Gar	1908	Q.A.	5/09 ANNIE
GRM	12/06 Milan	Riv	_____
GSP	9/08	RPP	_____
G.V.	_____	Ross	04/07 (ann)
Har	_____	S.C.	_____
JPCP	_____	St.A.	_____
KEN	_____	St.J	_____
K.L.	_____	St.Joa	_____
K.M.	_____	St.M.	_____
L.H.	_____	Sgt	_____
LO	_____	T.II.	_____
Lyn	_____	TLLO	_____
L.V.	8/07	T.M.	_____
McC	_____	T.T.	_____
McG	_____	Ven	_____
McQ	_____	Vets	_____
	_____	VP	_____
	_____	Wed	_____
	_____	W.L.	_____

ECHOES FROM THE PAST

ECHOES FROM THE PAST

Catherine Vincent

CHIVERS
THORNDIKE

This Large Print edition is published by BBC Audiobooks Ltd, Bath, England and by Thorndike Press®, Waterville, Maine, USA.

Published in 2004 in the U.K. by arrangement with the author.

Published in 2004 in the U.S. by arrangement with Juliet Burton Literary Agency.

U.K. Hardcover   ISBN 0–7540–7706–3   (Chivers Large Print)
U.K. Softcover   ISBN 0–7540–7707–1   (Camden Large Print)
U.S. Softcover   ISBN 0–7862–5946–9   (Nightingale)

The text of this Large Print edition is unabridged.
Other aspects of the book may vary from the original edition.

Set in 16 pt. New Times Roman.

Printed in Great Britain on acid-free paper.

British Library Cataloguing in Publication Data available

Library of Congress Cataloging-in-Publication Data

Vincent, Catherine, 1951–
    Echoes from the past / by Catherine Vincent.
        p.   cm.
    ISBN 0–7862–5946–9 (lg. print : sc : alk. paper)
    1. Married women—Fiction. 2. Marital conflict—Fiction.
    3. Large type books. I. Title.
    PR6072.I48E28 2004
    823'.914—dc22   2003061635

CHAPTER ONE

In every direction lay the moors, an empty tangle of bracken and gorse stretching as far as the eye could see. At the best of times, it could be an eerie place, with its loneliness and the unearthly whispering of the wind. But at twilight, and winter twilight at that, it was a brave soul who ventured out there alone.

Not that Jessica intended venturing out. She stood at the cottage window, a slight figure with a grave, unsmiling face, hardly visible beside the heavy velvet curtain, silently watching the shadows creep down from the hills. Shivering slightly, she drew her thick, red fleece even closer about her shoulders. Snow was hovering, hanging heavy and low in the darkening sky, but it wasn't the cold making her tremble. She'd been restless, uneasy all day, and she lifted a slender hand to her brow, trying to brush the hateful images away.

'It's not true,' she insisted, 'I'm safe here. He doesn't know where I am.'

Back in London, among all the bustle and noise, her sister's cottage had seemed the ideal place to rest, to recuperate, but Jessica hadn't reckoned on being there alone. Fiona would be with her, Fiona, her older sister, always so calm and unflappable, who had been more like a mother since they'd lost both their parents many years ago.

However, Fiona, a successful solicitor in the North of England, wasn't there. She had driven to Heathrow early that morning to meet a client, and Jessica herself had waved her away.

'Of course I can manage alone for a night,' she'd reassured Fiona with an airy wave of the hand. 'Go and meet your client, Fee. I'll be fine.'

'You're sure?' Fee had asked anxiously, but Jessica only laughed.

'Of course.'

She'd grinned, shaking her head, though now that darkness was falling, she wasn't nearly so certain. Somehow, she couldn't rid herself of the feeling that there was something lurking outside, just out of sight, watching her every move.

Once or twice, just for a moment, she was sure she'd caught sight of a movement, glimpsed for a second in the corner of her eye, or a shadow that wasn't quite still. But when she'd looked again, quickly turning her head to catch it, it was gone.

Commonsense told her it couldn't be true, but commonsense wasn't uppermost in her mind. Fear stole through her, formless, unreal, setting the hairs on the back of her neck on end.

'For heaven's sake, Jessica,' she admonished sharply, 'just one night alone. Surely you can manage that.'

Momentarily chastened, she tore herself away from the window and for about the tenth time in no more than an hour, she found herself going to check on the baby lying in his crib. Carefully, she re-arranged the covers about his tiny form, a soft smile touching her lips.

He was perfectly all right, of course. Still. fast asleep in his place by the fire, downy head on the pillow, his fists curled tight, he hadn't stirred since she'd last peeped down at him, which was hardly surprising, since it had only been a matter of minutes.

'Sleep on, my son,' she whispered. 'You're quite safe.'

Maybe the sight of her baby, obviously safe and well, might have finally settled his young mother's overstretched nerves. Straightening up, she decided to make herself a coffee, give herself something practical to do, but before she was halfway across the room, she froze, listening, and she was right. The wind was definitely rising.

The sound was muted at first, a mere sigh whispering around the rough cottage wall, but it rose in intensity even as she listened, rattling the windows in their frames, throwing gusts of early snow against the glass. Swiftly, she drew the curtains, shutting out the dismal scene. Very carefully, she took a deep breath, and then exhaled it slowly, steadying herself. She was inside, safe in the cottage. There was nothing for her to fear. A fire glowed in the old stone fireplace, the firelight winking and flickering on the burnished brasses strung out along the ceiling beams, and a television chattered away in the background, filling the room with its friendly noise.

At last, commonsense seemed to be taking command, and humming resolutely under her breath, she took herself off to the kitchen to switch on the kettle. She made the coffee strong and sweet, and carried it through to the living-room. Turning up the sound on the TV, she tried to lose herself in the rather dated film, but the more she tried to make herself watch, the more incomprehensible it became. Finally, she gave up altogether.

She was never going to make sense of it anyway. Perhaps she could read instead. There was a magazine on the table she hadn't had a chance to look at yet, and she picked it up, flicking the pages open with forced interest. A sudden, sharp noise from the garden brought her trembling to her feet, all thoughts of reading banished.

It had sounded like the crash of a gate swinging shut in the wind, and ice seemed to invade her veins. After several seconds, ears straining to hear, a shudder ran through her slender frame. With a terrible, stark certainty, she knew someone was outside in the garden. Ashen-faced, she listened again, to the

4

unmistakable sound of feet crunching along the gravel path from the road, but the sharp knock on the door took her utterly by surprise.

'Who can it be on a night like this?' she whispered to herself, terrified.

On shaky legs, she crept into the hall, her heart playing leapfrog under her ribs. Half of her, the sensible part, told her not to be so stupid. It was hardly likely, it reasoned, that an intruder would knock, but the terrified half of her, the half that had pestered her all day, just wouldn't let go.

'Who is it?' she managed at last, her voice. little more than a croak, but the answer was snatched away by the wind.

The only thing Jessica could be certain of was that the caller was male. Her hand lifted towards the latch, but who knows how long she'd have stood here, unable to move, if the voice hadn't called out again? The words were still muffled and far from clear, but the tone was decidedly urgent, and in sudden, blind panic, the thought of an accident struck her.

Her heart contracted sharply, and she cried out, involuntarily, her voice thin with fear. The image of her sister, lying crumpled at the roadside, beyond help like her parents before her, was more than Jessica could bear.

'No, no,' she called out, shaking her head, and slowly, agonisingly slowly, she turned the key in the latch.

She'd only meant to open the door a

fraction, just enough to peep outside, but she'd reckoned without the wind. Scarcely had the door started to move, when it was torn out of her hands. There was nothing she could do to stop it, and before she had chance to grab it again, it was flung inward by the force of the blast, leaving nothing between her and the raging storm outside. A man's tall figure stood in the tiny porch. He turned at the sound of her audible gasp, his teeth gleaming white in a mirthless smile.

'Well, well, Jessica,' he said softly, 'aren't you going to invite me in? I've travelled for hours to get here.'

In cold, unbelievable horror, Jessica stared up at him as if the devil himself had appeared before her eyes.

'Hawke,' she babbled, almost incoherent with shock. 'Oh, no! It can't be, it can't be!'

'Oh, but it can, my dear Jess. It most surely can.'

Jessica wanted to cry out, but no words would come. Her voice was paralysed in her throat. Wildly, she snatched at the door, trying to shut out the sight of him, but he was too quick for her. Planting his palm flat on the surface, he bent his head until his eyes were glittering deep into hers.

'Now that wasn't very friendly, was it?' he queried, in a deep voice lacking in any warmth. 'Trying to shut me out on night like this, when I've travelled so far to get here?'

'Well, you've wasted your time,' Jessica flashed back, and she made one final leap at the door, but she couldn't budge it an inch.

'Have you quite finished?' he enquired, excessively polite.

'No,' she insisted, still refusing to admit her position was hopeless.

'Yes,' he corrected. 'We have things to discuss, but if you don't mind, I'd much rather do it inside.'

She reacted quickly, far too quickly, as it turned out. She didn't give herself time to think.

'There is nothing I have to say to you,' she told him sharply, 'and since there's no-one else to talk to, you may as well go home.'

Too late, she realised her mistake, seeing the expression of grim satisfaction lighting his face.

'So, there's no-one else here,' he said softly. 'That's even better than I hoped for. Now we can talk, uninterrupted.'

A chill fear clutched at her heart. She made a horrified movement away from him, but one glance into the dark face above her, and any appeal on her own behalf, died unspoken on her lips. She could expect no sympathy.

'Go away, Hawke, leave me alone,' she repeated, but he only smiled that wolfish smile of his.

'But I don't want to go away,' he informed her smoothly. 'I've only just got here, and we have far too much to talk about.'

Without further ado, he stepped over the threshold into the tiny hall. The door closed behind him, sharply, shutting out the noise of the wind still howling through the blustery, snow-filled air. At once, the silence inside seemed deeper, almost suffocating.

She was trapped, caught alone with the man she dreaded most in the whole world—Rufus Hawke Munro, eldest son of the Earl of Glen Marr.

With an imperious wave of his hand, he indicated towards the half-open living-room door. Gritting her teeth, she turned and led the way in. There was no earthly use in arguing the point any further, not now that he was inside, but her head was high, her features a rigidly-controlled mask.

'Well?' she demanded, throwing him a baleful glare, but he didn't spare her an answer at once.

He had crossed to stand in front of the fire, his great shoulders giving an almost imperceptible shudder, and she guessed he was well-nigh perished from the cold. But she didn't offer him a drink, or invite him to remove his dripping coat. Why should she, when he shouldn't be here at all?

Standing there, with the leaping flames highlighting the generous mouth, the determined chin, Hawke was, without doubt, what most people would call a handsome man.

He was known as Hawke to family and friends alike. The one name sufficed, even for lovers, Jessica reflected bitterly.

Stiffly, he turned, blue eyes regarding her watchfully with a direct, unwavering gaze. It was hard to believe that those selfsame eyes, now as hard as flints, had once softened with love whenever they looked at her. Hard to believe, maybe, but true nonetheless. Stubbornly, Jessica stared back, gritting her teeth against the unwelcome, bittersweet memory. She had a new life now, a life with the baby, a life Hawke had no part in.

'Cat got your tongue?' he asked at last, but she didn't deign to reply. 'Jess,' he began again, sounding more than a trifle displeased by her continued lack of response, and this time she shrugged.

'I've already told you Hawke,' she said quietly, 'we have nothing to say to each other. Go home and leave me alone.'

'Just like that?' he ground out through clenched teeth.

'That was always your trouble,' she countered at once, in a voice as frigid as ice. 'You could never take no for an answer.'

'Enough,' he snapped, and took a step towards her.

He moved with surprising grace for one so large and powerful, crossing the floor between them with long, swift strides. Jessica's heart leaped like a startled deer at his approach. She

9

didn't want him to touch her, didn't want to feel those long, lean fingers again, warm on her skin, and it took every ounce of her self-control to prevent her legs from betraying her completely and retreating in front of him.

He came to a stop before her, only inches away. Then, with a movement so sudden, so swift, it caught her off guard, his hand shot out, closing over the delicate bones of her shoulder.

'Good grief,' he exclaimed, looking her over with horrified eyes. 'What on earth have you done to yourself? Have you been ill?'

'No, Hawke, let me alone.'

She would never tell him how much she'd suffered, how sick she'd been, but he wasn't even listening. He turned her body in front of him, seeing her properly for the first time. Putting out a hand to lift her chin, the better to scrutinise her face, he frowned, eyes narrowed, noting the pallor of the once-creamy skin, the smudges beneath eyes that looked too large and dark for her face.

She was only a small figure for all her twenty years, just over five feet tall and delicately slim, with a waterfall of thick, fair hair and the fragile grace of a gazelle. With her oval face and soft, sweet mouth, she could have been mistaken for a girl several years her junior, and she often was by people who didn't know her, but the illusion rarely lasted long. She was an independent young woman, bright and bubbly with the joys of living. Or at least, she sighed, she had been, until her life had been changed for ever by this insufferable man.

'Jess,' he repeated, his voice sharp with shock, 'what on earth have you been doing to yourself?'

'Nothing,' she insisted, glaring up at him with dark, defiant eyes.

'Nothing?' he reiterated. 'Do you think I'm a fool? You were always small, slim, but never so pale. You haven't been away so long that I've forgotten a single line or curve of you.'

Wordlessly, she shook her head, her heart racing erratically into overdrive. He had no right to remember, no right to tell her that he remembercd, not anymore.

Smiling, but with eyes like pebbles, he bent his head until his gaze was glowering on a level with hers.

'Answer me, Jess. I want to know,' he whispered again.

Again, Jessica shook her head. The troubled pregnancy and the agony of her son's birth, the complications that followed, almost claiming her life for good, weren't for Hawke's ears.

'There's nothing to tell,' she repeated obstinately.

With a muffled expletive, he turned his gaze heavenward, vexation hardening the line of his mouth. But before he could move, before he could say another word, and as if to answer his question, the baby began to cry in his crib. For what seemed like an eternity, the world stood still, frozen in that one small moment. Only the baby's wails, rising in a thin crescendo of sound, broke through the hush that had fallen within the cottage walls.

Mutely, she shifted in Hawke's grip, desperate to go to her son, but Hawke didn't release his hold upon her.

'I see,' he hissed. 'So that's it.'

He moved across the room, taking Jessica with him, pausing only to stare into the child's crumpled little face.

'Please, Hawke,' she said, 'let me pick him up. He's hungry.'

'He? It's a boy, then?'

'Yes, it's a boy.'

At that, he let her go, and Jessica lifted the crying infant into her arms. She rocked him to her, murmuring words of comfort against his downy head, until his screams finally diminished and died away, leaving a silence behind them more terrible than any words could possibly be.

'Jess,' Hawke began, his voice ominously quiet, 'look at me.'

'The baby,' she began, prevaricating wildly, but he shook his head.

'Never mind the baby,' he said, 'just look at me when I ask. Yours?'

'Of course,' she countered, tossing her head with a brave attempt at defiance. 'All mine,' she added, chin held at a proud angle.

He held her gaze for a moment, searching its stormy depths, then his eyebrows lifted a fraction.

'All yours?' he queried. 'I suppose I had nothing to do with it.'

Jessica couldn't speak, couldn't utter a sound. Her world was falling apart, crushed between the fingers of this man.

'Just look at him, Jess,' the relentless voice persisted, 'and tell me he's not my son.'

She couldn't, of course. The likeness was too marked to refute. Briefly, Hawke waited, but when she still didn't reply, he continued his onslaught.

'And that's my ring you still have on your finger. So, legally, morally, in every sense of the word, this baby is mine.'

His voice was silky-soft, but with such an edge of flat certainty that fear clogged Jessica's throat. She clutched the baby's tiny body closer.

'Oh, my poor baby,' she murmured, her voice scarcely audible. 'My poor little Paul.'

'Paul?'

Hawke's query was swift, and decisively, he shook his head.

'Oh, no,' he said, 'that's no name for a Munro of Glen Marr. We'll call him Gavin,' he added, after a moment's thought. 'Gavin, another hawk.'

With those few, short words, he dismissed

all her hopes, her fragile dreams of a new life, a life without him. Automatically, she opened her mouth to protest, but the words died on her lips at the sight of that granite expression.

'My son,' he breathed, 'and you didn't think to tell me?'

She couldn't find the words to explain that there hadn't been anything to tell him, not when she'd left. Besides, what was the point? She knew he would never believe her.

'Well,' he shrugged, 'divorce is out of the question now.'

Abruptly, the blood drained from her face, leaving it drawn and paper white. She could guess where this was leading, and she didn't want to hear.

'I don't know what you mean,' she flung out.

His eyes narrowed in faint disbelief, his regard piercing as it scrutinised her mutinous expression.

'You know exactly what I mean,' he insisted. 'We have to go back to Glen Marr, all three of us, and like you say, I won't take no for an answer.'

Still she couldn't believe he really meant what he said, in spite of the relentless expression carved on his handsome features. Angrily, she pulled away, refusing to accept a truth that was staring her straight in the face.

'I want a divorce,' she repeated. 'You know that. You must have had the papers by now.'

Sheer bravado kept her eyes on his face, her

features a mask, trying to hide her raging emotions. But if she'd hoped to get under his guard, she'd failed. One eyebrow rose slightly, but his voice was surprisingly even.

'Of course,' he allowed, inclining his head, 'but what did you think would happen? Just a breathing space, a time to think, that's all you said. Then out of the blue, I receive a solicitor's letter, demanding a divorce I had never agreed to. Did you honestly believe I wouldn't come?'

A thread of contempt appeared in his tone, and her lips quivered in spite of all her attempts to control them.

'Oh, no,' she sighed, recalling all the long, weary hours, the watching, the waiting. 'I knew you'd come, I've been half-expecting you all day.'

'Then you know I'm taking you back to Glen Marr.'

Her initial instinct was to scream. She didn't want to go anywhere with him, let alone back to Glen Marr. The past was the past, gone, for ever.

Somehow, she had to make him understand.

'I can't come to Glen Marr,' she insisted. 'It didn't work before, and it won't work now.'

'Very well, Jessica, if that's what you want, so be it.'

It wasn't what she expected, this sudden capitulation, and an icy suspicion filled her with dread.

'You'll go?' she breathed, not believing him for a second.

'Oh, I'll go,' he assured her coldly, 'You can stay in London, if that's what you're set on. Go back to university, get your divorce, but I'm taking my son to Glen Marr, where he belongs.'

With that, he plucked the sleeping baby deftly from her arms. Any last, lingering doubt that Hawke would carry out his threat to the letter died at that moment. One glance into those set features was more than enough to convince her.

'I'll come,' she cried. 'I promise I'll come. Just give me my baby.'

She would have promised him anything in that moment, anything at all, and he must have heard the desperation spilling into her voice. Pausing, he glanced down at her, at the great dark eyes and the beseeching, trembling mouth, and he shrugged.

'Very well,' he conceded, 'but be quick. We have a long way to go.'

It couldn't exactly be called an encouraging invitation, not that Jessica cared tuppence about details like that. All that mattered now was to stay with her son.

'I'm ready,' she began, but he cut her words short.

'It's a long journey. Surely you'll need something for Gavin.'

She wouldn't argue, wouldn't dream of

16

crossing him now, not while he held her baby in his arms. In a veritable fever of haste, she fled to the bedroom and threw a few belongings into the bottom of an overnight bag, scarcely registering what she was doing. She filled another with things for her baby.

'Hawke,' she called, closing the zip, 'are you still there?'

There was no answer, and Jessica's heart contracted with fear. There had never been a fear like it, even in her darkest moments, and she flew into the hall like a madman, but he was in the little living-room, fitting the baby carefully into his car seat, and he straightened up as she shot towards him.

'Is something the matter?' he enquired, frowning, with what she thought was singular understatement, but she shook her head.

Arguing with him would have to come later. Besides, the sudden relief made her feel quite lightheaded, causing her head to swim. She'd been prone to fainting during her pregnancy, especially in the latter few weeks, and she didn't want it happening again now. Quickly, she stiffened her back and kept herself upright, upright and walking.

'Shall I take him now?' she queried, her mind on one thing and one thing only, her baby.

'How can you?' Hawke demurred. 'You don't look strong enough to carry yourself. I'll take him to the car. You'd better write Fiona a

17

note. We don't want her panicking when she gets back, involving the police even.'

To Jessica, involving the police sounded like the best idea yet. Perhaps they would be able to talk some sense into him, but she did as he said. She couldn't let Fiona walk into an empty house without a word of explanation. A letter would be bad enough. Total silence would be unbearable. So, taking a sheet of paper from the sideboard drawer, she scribbled a few brief lines to her sister, that she'd left the cottage with Hawke. That was all she said, hoping the lack of detail would alert Fiona, tell her that all wasn't well.

If only, Jessica reflected bitterly. Fiona would probably think this was the happy ending she'd always been hoping for. She liked Hawke, had always liked Hawke. Charmed by his innate courtesy, his caring, the ready humour always bubbling beneath the surface, ready to break out in easy laughter, she thought her sister was mad to let him go.

'You live with him then,' Jessica remembered snapping.

'Just give me the chance,' had been Fee's wry response. 'Unfortunately, the man only has eyes for you.'

Well, he hasn't got eyes for me now, she noted grimly. That time had long gone. It was his male pride that had brought him here. No-one crossed Hawke and got away with it.

He took the letter from her, scanning it

swiftly, his brows drawn into a faint frown, but he seemed satisfied, and in his firm, sloping hand, he added a couple of lines of his own, at the bottom. Then he folded the paper and propped it carefully on the mantelpiece, where Fiona would see it as soon as she got home.

With shaky hands, she placed the guard in front of the fire and settled the logs, making them safe. As she straightened, the clock chimed out into the silence, its suddenness making her jump. Its cracked, old voice whirred out eight times in all, before it fell silent again. Eight o'clock, she reflected, only eight o'clock. It seemed like a lifetime had passed.

'Ready?' Hawke queried.

Acutely conscious of his eyes upon her, her chin lifted a fraction. Determination not to give him the satisfaction of seeing her cry kept the threatening tears at bay. Now was a time for being clear-headed, for thinking straight, not for giving way to her emotions.

'Ready,' she affirmed, and without so much as a backward glance, she followed him out of the door.

CHAPTER TWO

Outside, the night had a strange feeling about it, surprisingly muffled and still, and with a kind of tired disbelief, Jessica saw that the storm had blown itself out. Nothing was left of the driving snow except a satin-like sheen on the surface of the road.

'Come,' Hawke said, putting out his free hand to take her arm, and with a half-stifled sigh, Jessica allowed him to lead her to the car.

But her legs still didn't belong to her, and her head wasn't much better. Several times she almost stumbled. Only Hawke's hand on her arm, firm and strong, kept her steady.

'All right?' he asked, and she shrugged, unwilling to admit to even a chink in her armour.

If it wasn't for him, she wouldn't be out there at all, facing a journey she could do without. Things had changed. They didn't belong together, not any more. She didn't belong at Glen Marr. Why couldn't he see that?

Jessica sighed faintly, trying to keep the intrusive memory at bay. If only she hadn't taken that vacation job. If only she'd stayed at home. But she had taken it, and the images were as crisp and clear as ever.

She'd been a student, at a loose end on her

first Easter vacation from medical school. When her two best friends had found holiday jobs in the Scottish Highlands, she'd leaped at the chance to go with them.

'It's a holiday lodge complex on the edge of a lake,' Penny had said.

'A loch,' Laura corrected, 'part of the Glen Marr estate.'

'Perhaps we'll meet the earl,' Jessica put in, grinning.

'Don't be silly,' her friends had scoffed. 'Got to be seventy at least.'

'Maybe he has a son.'

He had two, to be more precise. The old earl had married late, she'd discovered, and he was more than happy to retire in his beloved highlands, leaving the family business in the hands of his sons.

Alastair, the younger, was a farmer at heart, married and raising his family on the land. Hawke was the businessman, tough and commanding, expanding his interests into more than the range of organic produce the estate was so famous for. Forestry, tourism, sales and marketing were all added to the business, with himself as the formidable, larger-than-life head of the empire.

'Get in the car.'

Hawke's voice intruded suddenly into her thoughts, dragging her back to the present. But typically, he didn't wait to see if she could manage alone.

With scarcely an effort, he lifted her bodily up the high step of the gleaming black Range Rover waiting at the edge of the road, and she had to put up with his help with an unwilling, teeth-clenching grace.

The quiet inside the car was welcome, the quiet and the warmth. But Jessica couldn't relax and enjoy them.

'The baby' she insisted, a catch in her voice, and without a word, Hawke placed the carry seat on her lap.

For long, long moments, he watched. His eyes narrowed as she rocked the small body to her, holding him close, snuffling in the sweet, warm baby scent of him.

He opened his mouth, as if to say more, but evidently thought better of it, and she didn't argue when he took the car seat from her, strapping it safely on the back seat. Then shutting the passenger door with an abrupt snap, he went round to his own side of the car and slid into the driver's seat.

'It's a long way,' he added. 'You might as well get some rest.'

'I'm not tired,' she lied valiantly.

'Please yourself,' he shrugged, his expression impassive, and he started the engine, ready to move away.

The vehicle swept off, leaving the cottage behind, and the old, familiar feeling of dread caught at Jessica's heart again, bringing her out in a sick, cold sweat. In sheer panic, her hand flew to the door handle. She wanted to throw herself out of the car, before they'd gone too far, anything to avoid going back to Glen Marr. But how could she, with her baby strapped in the back seat? So she subsided, chewing hard on her bottom lip to try to stop it from trembling.

She had to go, had to fall in with Hawke's plans for the baby's sake, at least for the moment, and if he'd noticed the small, distracted movement beside him, he certainly didn't let on.

The car picked up speed, eating up the miles through the wintry night, and Jessica made herself sink back into the cushiony seat. Hawke was right, she had to rest. Every ounce of her strength, such as it was, had to be scraped together to face the journey ahead, not to mention the fight to follow, for a fight there was certainly going to be.

She had no idea how long they'd been going, sitting in silence, but it couldn't have been far before the baby started to cry. Just a thready wail for attention at first, it soon blossomed into a full-blown scream of distress when it was ignored, and Jessica's heart sank. It was past his feeding time, by half-an-hour or so, and nothing else would quieten him this time.

'He's hungry,' she explained dully.

Hawke didn't speak, he merely pulled into a layby at the edge of the empty road.

'Then you'd better feed him,' he said grimly.

A warmth that was nothing to do with the car's excellent heating system suffused her cheeks with sudden colour. The thought of uncovering herself, in front of Hawke, set her teeth unbearably on edge. Such intimacy wasn't any part of her plans, even if they were still married, and she gazed up at him, dark eyes appalled.

'Now?' she queried, aghast.

'Of course, now,' he returned, his tone edged with exasperation. 'Can you suggest a better time?'

She couldn't, of course, and it was breaking her heart to ignore the baby's desperate cries.

'Surely you're not shy of me,' he demanded, the penny finally dropping, and his voice took on a note of incredulity. 'You're my wife,' he reminded her softly, his eyebrows raised. 'This baby is mine as well.'

He unstrapped the child from his seat and thrust the tiny bundle into her arms. At once, the baby ceased its cries and began questing hungrily against her. Jessica fumbled with the zipper of her fleece jacket, then the buttons on her blouse. She couldn't deny him any longer, so she finally lifted the child close, allowing the hungry little mouth to feed.

She was acutely conscious of Hawke's eyes, watching silently. Surreptitiously, she threw her husband a sideways glance from beneath the dark curtain of her discreetly lowered lashes, and found his eyes were still fixed on her face, disconcertingly cool and direct.

'Was it so very bad, having the baby?' he enquired.

'It was difficult,' she admitted softly.

There was no point in saying otherwise. Her pallor, her weakness, the distinct loss of weight would tell him that much at least.

'That means it must have been awful,' he sighed, and she half-smiled.

He had always known her too well.

'Maybe,' she shrugged.

'But you're all right now?' he queried, and she nodded.

'I'm OK,' she agreed.

It was ridiculous to feel so embarrassed, she tried to tell herself. He was the child's father, just as he said, and she did her best to relax. But a giant quiver ran through her when he put out a hand, moving the strands of her hair to give himself a better view of his son's small face pressed contentedly against her. The touch of those long fingers made her uneasy, making her flesh tingle in a way she'd much rather forget, bringing back images she didn't want to recall. She shifted in her seat, but she didn't utter a word.

At long last, after what seemed like hours, the baby finally finished his feed and he fell almost immediately into a well-fed sleep. Jessica made him comfortable and settled him back in his seat.

'Well, you'll soon get strong, back at Glen Marr,' Hawke reflected aloud, restarting the car's powerful engine. 'The mountain air, the loch, all the fresh, wholesome food you can eat.'

Jessica stared out of the window, trying to blot out the pictures his words were bringing back. Glen Marr—the great Scottish estate, high in the mountains, home to the Munro family for untold generations. It had captured her imagination from the first moment she'd set eyes on it.

It had been a clear spring morning when the bus had dropped off her and her friends. Jessica could see it still. The memory was as vivid as ever; not one tiny detail, not one touch of colour had faded. The three teenage girls had stood at the side of the road, tired from the long journey. Only Jessica's eyes had strayed irresistibly towards the main house.

'Just look at that,' she breathed.

Glimpsed through the trees, it was typically baronial, grey and turreted like some long-lost Celtic castle glimpsed through the mists of history. She half-expected some kilted hero to appear, playing his pipes on the battlements.

'Not for the likes of us,' Laura snorted, and, pointing towards the modern estate offices, she added, 'That's where we belong.'

'Looks good to me,' Penny shrugged. 'Give me my home comforts any day of the week.'

It had been hard work for the three young

friends at Glen Marr, but there was time for pleasure as well. Jessica had taken to riding out every day, trail blazing through the forest on a sturdy chestnut cob, and it was on one such outing that destiny took a hand. She ran into Hawke.

Tall and whipcord strong, riding his eye-catching thoroughbred mare, Jessica had never met a man like him, and it seemed that Hawke had never seen anyone quite like Jessica. One look at the fair, elfin-like girl and he'd lost no time in asking her out to dinner. After that, they'd spent every spare moment together, and the rest as they say, was history.

She had married him in the summer, on a hot day in July, barely three months after they'd first met, and still a couple of months short of her nineteenth birthday. Like the proverbial dream come true, it seemed nothing could cloud their happiness.

Jessica bit her lip in the dark interior of the car, and stole a swift glance at the silent man at her side. She had loved him so much. Even the mere touch of his hand, his voice whispering her name in the darkness, had been enough, more than enough, to set her trembling, every nerve in her body quivering finely on end. How on earth had it all gone so wrong?

His eyes seemed fixed on the road, unheeding, or so it appeared, but he turned his head, just as she'd known he would.

'Well, little wife?' he asked softly.

Immediately, she looked away, avoiding his gaze. Little wife, indeed! He was still talking as if he owned her, and she shifted resentfully in her seat. It wasn't Hawke who'd been forced to give up a university place. It wasn't Hawke who'd said goodbye to a career.

'Being my wife is all you'll ever need,' he'd insisted doggedly, over and over again.

He had wanted to protect her, take care of her, grant her every wish, but Jessica was a modern girl, hoping for a career, a life with some personal freedom to it, and after a time, it had all proved too much. She'd felt smothered, wrapped in cotton wool. She wasn't able to breathe.

He'd actually forbidden her to go back to her studies. Forbidden! In this day and age! Jessica had scarcely been able to credit it, and when she'd gone ahead, when he'd found out she'd been in touch with her tutor again, asking advice, making enquiries, an ungovernable rage had erupted.

'You're my wife,' he'd reminded her savagely, 'and that means being here with me, looking after my home, taking some note of what I want.'

'And you're my husband,' she'd flashed back. 'Doesn't that mean taking some note of my feelings, too? Or does that rule only apply to me?'

It was the final straw. She just couldn't live

the way he wanted her to, constrained, like a bird in a cage. Soon they were arguing, all the time, about everything, everything and nothing, and barely twelve months into their marriage, she persuaded Hawke to let her take a trip to London.

It was their only hope, she'd told him. They needed breathing space, just for a few weeks, and she'd really belicved it at the time. Then she'd discovered about the baby, and it had changed everything.

'Are you sure this is what you want?' her sister had asked, her face concerned, as the weeks gradually turned into months.

But Jessica had only gritted hcr teeth. Escape from Glen Marr was the only answer. She couldn't walk back into Hawke's cage now. Her independence would go out of the door for good.

'Hawke and I want different things from life,' she'd insisted.

'But the baby,' Fee had queried.

'I'll tell him when it's all over.'

And Jessica meant it. She would tell Hawke about his child. That wasn't in question, but not yet, she'd prevaricated. Not until things are settled between us, when he knows I'm not coming back, baby or no baby.

Almost from the first, there'd been problems with the pregnancy—a birth that came too early and unending hours of labour had truly put her life in peril. Only emergency surgery finally put an end to Jessica's sufferings. Even then, for her it had been touch and go. Her son, two months premature but as strong as his powerful father, had thrived, and almost a month to the day, they'd finally been allowed out of hospital.

Still wretchedly weak, she'd jumped at the chance of staying with Fiona. Her solicitor had finally contacted Hawke, and she wasn't too keen on being alone in London. She knew what his reaction would be, and she hadn't been wrong.

Sudden lights illuminated the interior of the car, drawing her gaze back to the window. They'd reached a service area, but she shook her head at the suggestion they should stop. Later perhaps, she demurred, when the baby needed another feed, and she drooped back into her seat. Hawke, it seemed, had given up any attempt at conversation, but she had to say something to fill the uneasy void.

'Is everything all right at Glen Marr?' she enquired, and he gave a shrug.

'The same,' he returned.

'As successful, as ever,' she commented tartly, thinking that even the departure of a wife wouldn't cause a hiccup in Hawke's business affairs.

He raised an eyebrow at her tone, mouth set in a thin line, and Jessica subsided into silence once more. Arguing with him wasn't worth the hassle, not here, anyway, not now. But Hawke decided he wanted to talk.

'Mother will be pleased to see Gavin,' he began, 'and so will Father. He's heir to the Glen Marr estate, after all.'

'The latest of a long line,' she interrupted in acid tones.

'Of course.'

The flat assurance in his voice set Jessica's teeth decidedly on edge. The man hadn't changed one bit. Surely even he must know he couldn't keep her against her will for ever.

'And what about me?' she demanded fiercely.

Hawke glanced briefly towards her, one brow quirked in her direction, but his tone didn't change one bit.

'You, my dear Jess,' he returned smoothly, 'will do as you're told.'

'And if I won't?'

'I don't want to fight you for custody of Gavin, but I will if I have to.'

The veiled threat was obvious, and for an instant, a chill fear invaded Jessica's heart. He looked so very sure of himself.

'Most courts would give a child to its mother,' she countered.

'Not automatically, not nowadays,' he contradicted. 'Fathers have rights, too, and I have money, position. I could fight you through every court in the land, and I'm not entirely without influence.'

He was painting a picture so awful, so

31

terrifyingly possible, it scared her half out of her mind.

'I'd fight,' she vowed. 'I'd get him back.'

For timeless moments, he didn't speak, his eyes narrowed and watchful under frowning brows. Then he pulled over to the side of the road.

'Not for weeks, months even,' he assured her, 'and all that time, he'd be living with me,' then abruptly, he leaned across to throw open the passenger door, letting in a rush of cold, rain-laden air. 'But if that's what you want,' he added grimly, 'you might as well go now: I'll see you in court.'

She didn't speak. She didn't have to. The answer was etched on her face. Nodding, he pulled the door shut, steering the powerful vehicle back on to the road.

'Very well,' he said, 'but remember, I gave you the choice.'

Some choice, but Jessica held her tongue. My time will come, she promised herself, hands clutched to fists in her lap, and she sank back into her seat, every muscle in her body frozen to ice.

The rest of the journey north was a nightmare. Her mind wouldn't stop spinning, tormented by the same pictures, the same harsh words, over and over again. Just before dawn, they reached Inverness and drove in silence through the deserted streets, turning at last on to the country road climbing the final, fateful miles to Glen Marr. Jessica had never expected to see it again, and she watched with a sinking feeling of dread as the first light of day, luminous and still, rose behind the dark silhouette of its hills.

The sound of the tyres, scrunching along a wet gravel drive, told her they had finally reached the house, and feeling more dead than alive, she managed to drag herself out of the car. Close to, the place was truly imposing. Tall and grey, standing in acres of rolling parkland, its thick stone walls sprawled out before her. Twenty bedrooms and almost as many living areas made it a home of impressive proportions.

Wood-panelled walls and the gleaming parquet floors, scattered here and there with expensive Persian carpets, added to its rich sense of history. Even the paintings, lining the broad sweep of the carved oak staircase, portraits of former lords and ladies of the house for the most part, seemed to agree, looking down on the subtle mix of modern, comfortable living and ancestral tradition with approving eyes.

Jessica hadn't stepped inside the house for months, and she stood for a moment in the entrance hall, breathing in the familiar scent of real wax polish and fresh, hothouse flowers grown especially on the estate. She glimpsed the sturdy figure of a girl in a fitted dress of crisp green cotton, no more than seventeen or eighteen years old at the most. But the young face was strange to her, and she started forward, wondering vaguely if she was a new maid. But suddenly, without warning, Jessica's legs crumpled beneath her and she fell, too weak to manage another step.

Dimly, she heard the maid's scream, then Hawke's voice calling her name, and powerful hand slipped under her shoulders. The whole room tilted at a strange, unnatural angle, and when it righted itself again, she was high in her husband's arms.

'Hawke,' she sighed, putting up a hand to touch his face.

'Go to sleep,' he answered abruptly.

The world was ebbing and flowing about her, and for one long, dreadful moment the last year seemed to slide away, as if it had never happened, and Hawke was in charge of her life once more.

'My baby,' she whispered.

But her mind was darkening, letting go again. Her consciousness diminished into a tiny bead at the back of her mind. Then it blinked, finally, into nothingness. Mercifully, she had no knowledge at all of reaching the bedroom, of being placed, as helpless as any child, on to the waiting bed.

Strong hands divested her of her garments, but still, she wasn't able to open her eyes.

Only the sound of voices, disembodied, unreal, shimmered unseen in the thick, velvet-dark air. One was Margaret, Hawke's mother, sounding sharp and very angry indeed.

'Good grief,' she was saying, 'what on earth have you done to her, Rufus?'

Only his parents ever called him by that part of his name.

'Me? I haven't done anything to her,' came Hawke's reply, angry, too, and on the defensive.

'But she looks half-dead. Where's her coat, and did she eat before she came out?'

His silence was more eloquent than any words, and even to Jessica's ears, his answer, when it came, sounded decidedly sheepish.

'I don't know,' he admitted finally.

'I see,' his mother returned, her voice dripping acid. 'Really, Rufus, I could box your ears, big as you are.'

'Mother!'

'Don't "mother" me,' Margaret snapped back. 'I know you too well, my son. You're not telling me Jessica left like this of her own free will.'

Again, there was no immediately reply.

'I thought not,' Margaret snorted. 'Once you get the bit between your teeth, nothing can stop you. I don't know where you get it from,' she added plaintively. 'Your father's such a gentle man.'

'Work it out for yourself,' Hawke muttered, and his mother rounded on him at once.

'Don't be so cheeky,' she retorted, 'or I will

35

box your ears.'

'Mother,' Hawke growled again, but he said no more.

His hands continued, their work, removing Jessica's clothing, pulling some kind of garment over her head before settling her. helpless body under the quilt. A few wayward strands of hair had settled across her face, and she felt his fingertips brush them aside. Brisk, they were, and efficient, but not entirely devoid of gentleness.

'She's coming round, thank goodness,' Margaret breathed. 'You'd better make yourself scarce, Rufus. We don't want her fainting again.'

'Thanks for the vote of confidence,' Hawke returned sarcastically.

'We'll see what she has to say,' his mother insisted, and Jessica sighed.

She had an ally at Glen Marr. Margaret understood. Gradually, the pale slither of light under her eyelids expanded, and she blinked as the room swam painfully back into focus. Margaret was bending over her.

'Lie still, my dear,' she said softly. 'Rufus is going downstairs now, to ask Helen to bring up the baby, aren't you, my son?'

For just a moment, Jessica caught a glimpse of him, grim-faced and unsmiling, paused in the doorway. Then he was gone, and the sound of his footsteps faded as he followed his mother's instructions to take himself down the stairs. Within minutes, the same young girl she'd encountered so briefly in the hall brought the baby to the door. She threw Jessica a glance, round-eyed with curiosity, before being ushered out of the room. The baby was awake now, and beginning to fret again to be fed. Carefully, Margaret lifted the carrier and brought it to the bed.

'He's so beautiful,' she breathed.

Jessica's smile held a tinge of sadness. She hadn't thought about Margaret when she'd kept the baby a secret, or the earl for that matter. She hadn't really thought about anyone. A clean break, a swift end to a relationship gone sour, had seemed for the best. But now she wondered if she could have found a better way. Perhaps, then, even Hawke himself wouldn't have been so angry.

'I did love Hawke once,' she stammered, 'very much. But we rushed into things too fast, and sometimes, love alone just isn't enough.'

'No more,' Margaret broke in. 'Time for explanations later. Just take care of this young man. He looks as if he has a mighty appetite.'

A mighty appetite was an understatement, and only when the baby was settled again could Jessica even begin to think of her own needs. Cereal and a glass of orange juice were waiting on a tray, together with a boiled egg in a silver cup and slices of freshly-buttered bread. Suddenly, Jessica realised how hungry she was.

'Shall I take the baby,' Margaret asked softly, 'while you eat?'

Tenderly, her eyes filmed with unshed tears, Margaret balanced the tiny form close, smoothing the silky fluff on the baby's head with a hand that couldn't quite stop itself from shaking.

'He's a beautiful baby,' Margaret insisted again, and the ghost of a smile touched Jessica's lips.

'You wouldn't be just a mite prejudiced?' she teased gently, with the hint of the old sparkle gleaming in her eyes.

'Maybe a little,' Margaret admitted. 'He's another Rufus, without a doubt.'

Good grief, Jessica thought, pausing in eating her egg. Had she really produced another Hawke? Grimly, she took a bit of toast, her eyes on her son. Well, she consoled herself, admitting the likeness, as long as he doesn't inherit his father's outdated ideas about women as well as his looks.

Safe in her cocoon of warmth, with her baby asleep at her side, Jessica didn't stir from her bed for a full twenty-four hours, rousing herself only to see to the needs of her son. But while she slept, the storm roared into Glen Marr. After its brief respite, it had followed them north in all its ferocity. Swirling eerily through the trees in flurries of thick, white flakes, the snow came sweeping up to the very doorstep.

It fell all day long, heavy, white and impenetrable, forming great icy drifts in the gusting wind, and when it was finally spent, the drifts were piled crisp and cold, as high as the frosty windows. In the midst of it all, the house stood like a dark island in a drifting sea of white, but the sky still hung heavy and low with the promise of more falls to come, and the wind still howled, as keen as a knife, across the frozen landscape. To Jessica's horrified eyes, when she finally did wake up, all signs of her old, familiar world had vanished completely. The house seemed suddenly very alone.

Shivering slightly, she looked up into the threatening sky. There was no possible doubt about it. She was trapped. Glen Marr was cut off completely from the outside world, all roads impassable. Even the telephone wires would be down. No-one would get in or out of the village for days. Miserably, she slid back under the covers, pulling the duvet even farther up round her ears. She wanted no part of that cold, alien world. She'd stay where she was, thank you very much, safe in her own warm bed.

'It's no use doing that. You have to get up sometime.'

Hawke's voice broke into her thoughts, and she glowered over at him.

He had no right to be there.

'Can't you knock before barging in?' she demanded fiercely.

39

'Knock?'

He was leaning against the doorpost, casually dressed in a traditional Aran sweater, thick knit and heavy, pulled over immaculate beige cords. His air of confidence, lounging about in her bedroom, got under her skin.

'You heard,' she returned sharply.

His eyebrows lifted a fraction, as if he couldn't quite believe the evidence of his own ears, and his voice took on a faintly amused tone.

'Knock?' he repeated. 'In my own house, on my own bedroom door? What a quaint, outmoded sense of modesty you must have.'

He took a step towards her, his eyes hooded, their expression faintly mocking, and she shot to a sitting position, the quilt pulled up to her chin. She felt suddenly very vulnerable, lying in that huge bed, but she couldn't do anything about it while he was standing there with that speculative look on his face.

'Stay away,' she warned, a faint flush of pink touching her cheeks, but he didn't listen.

Instead, he sat down, right on the edge of the bed, far too close for her comfort, and very deliberately, he pulled the protecting duvet out from under her chin.

'Don't be so silly,' he said softly.

Angrily, she tried to prise the quilt from between his long fingers, but she was no match for his strength, and gritting her teeth, she finally gave up the unequal struggle.

'I'm not being silly,' she flung back. 'We're not married now, not in the proper sense.'

'But I don't remember agreeing to that,' he countered smoothly. 'So far as I'm concerned, our marriage vows were for life. Mine certainly were, and I expected yours to be the same. You knew that when you married me.'

'Go away,' she tried to insist.

'But you're my wife,' he murmured. 'And I mean my wife,' he promised huskily, 'in every possible sense of the word.'

CHAPTER THREE

Just for a second, Jessica was robbed entirely of the power of speech.

She stiffened feeling the brush of his fingers against her averted cheek horribly conscious of every wild beat of her heart.

'No,' she managed finally.

With devastating ease, he sat beside her, exuding charm from every pore. Horrified at her reaction, at the way every nerve leaped just to be near him, she tried to pull away. But she couldn't move, held in thrall by a magnetism, a feeling between them so intense that it took every ounce of her willpower not to lift her face to invite his kiss. Drawing in a long breath, she exhaled it slowly, and finally, resolutely, she lifted her eyes to meet his gaze. It was resting on her, gleaming with such compelling intensity that the colour was driven abruptly back into her cheeks.

'Maybe not just yet,' he allowed softly, 'but soon, my sweet, soon, we will be truly together again.'

Together? Had he honestly said together? Jessica shook her head. No matter what her traitorous heart was trying to tell her, so what if her love wasn't quite as dead as she'd hoped, they could hardly pick up the pieces again as if she'd never been away. He had to be mad to imagine that! Forcing her features into an expression of studied calm, she regarded him coolly as it she was giving his comments due consideration.

'Sorry to disappoint you,' she said finally, 'but I intend to be long gone by then, as soon as the roads are clear again.'

'We'll see.'

He smiled, finally rising to his feet again.

'We will,' she assured him, with a lift of her narrow shoulders.

She might be stuck in Glen Marr, but that was all. She had no intention of playing Hawke's wife. He chose to ignore her, but his eyes were glinting with humour as he turned at the door.

'See you at breakfast.'

'If I have to,' she conceded, then added briskly, 'but seriously, Hawke, we have to talk.'

'Seriously?'

His eyes never wavered from her solemn features, and she nodded. She was doing her best to be serious, though it wasn't easy, not under that piercing gaze. He looked quite formidable standing there, rugged and calmly self-assured, projecting an aura so full of himself that was positively daunting. But she refused to be pushed away from her purpose.

'Sometimes people make mistakes,' she began. 'We made a mistake. Now, we have to decide how to put things right.'

'A divorce, you mean?'

'Maybe . . . probably . . .'

She knew she was stammering, but she made herself go on.

'We have a child to consider now,' she continued softly.

'Surely a child means we should try again.'

His tone was so determined, so obviously lacking in any sign of compromise, that her resolve almost failed. It seemed an impossible task, trying to budge such an immovable rock of a man. She couldn't imagine Hawke giving way to anyone. But she couldn't agree, couldn't accept such a hopeless state of affairs, not and stay sane.

'No, Hawke,' she tried to insist, fighting desperately to keep her voice on an even keel. 'It was a mistake, you and I,' she added faintly, 'and I don't intend to live with it for ever.'

'What a pity,' he cut in, in a voice like iron, 'because I'm afraid you have no choice. You're not leaving here and taking my son.'

Jessica suppressed a slight shiver of apprehension. It was more than evident that he meant every word he said, and her blood chilled. But she kept her gaze steady.

'We'll see,' she said. 'Now, please, will you leave? I'd like to get up.'

She needed time to breathe, time to think, time away from Hawke's disturbing presence. Anyway, it had suddenly occurred to her that she could feel far less vulnerable dressed, up and out of bed, with Margaret around for

44

company.

'Good,' he shrugged, to her secret surprise.

She could hardly believe it. He was leaving. He was actually leaving. At once, she started to smile, her hopes beginning to rise, but they were swiftly dashed again.

'Oh, by the way,' he added, tossing the words over his shoulder almost as an afterthought, 'our son is being baptised today, so don't be long.'

Stunned, she could only gape at him with uncomprehending eyes. She must be mistaken. He couldn't have said what she'd thought he'd said.

'What?' she stuttered.

'Gavin is being baptised,' he repeated, very slowly.

'But the snow . . . the roads . . . I thought they were closed,' she stammered.

'So they are,' he agreed, 'but Glen Marr has its own chapel. You should know that, my sweet, unless, of course, you've forgotten our wedding.'

'I haven't forgotten,' she retorted bitterly.

As if she could! Their wedding, in the tiny place of worship high in one of the towers, was etched in her mind for ever.

'Good,' he repeated, 'then you know I mean it. Everything's arranged for this afternoon.'

'Don't rush into things, will you?'

Her voice was edged with unveiled sarcasm, her eyes sparking furiously.

45

'I don't want to wait,' he returned easily. 'The weather's bad enough now, but if it really closes in, we could be marooned for weeks. So,' he added, with the kind of mocking grin that really made her blood boil, 'get up, my sweet, and get dressed, before I have to see to it myself.'

'You wouldn't dare!'

She threw him a raging look, but her defiance almost failed as his eyebrow quirked.

'Try me,' he challenged softly.

In that split second, every old frustration, every tiny remembered slight, flared back into life. Resentment seared into her soul. Drat the man. He was doing it again, making her decisions, assuming he had the right.

'Please go,' she snapped.

If he didn't, she couldn't honestly answer for her temper.

'Not yet,' he answered, and turning back, he caught hold of the covers with a determined hand, throwing them aside to expose her slender form to the cold reality beyond her bed. 'I want to make quite sure you're up,' he added grimly.

It was hard for her to look dignified, lying there under his probing eyes, clad in nothing but one of his own silk pyjama tops. Large as it was, the material was so fine, so light, Jessica felt almost naked in it.

'Go away,' she repeated angrily.

Frowning, his eyes rested on her indignant

46

face, but thank goodness, he didn't attempt to touch her.

'Get up,' he commanded.

Resolutely, she stayed where she was, ignoring him. Who was he to order her about? But at her continued defiance, he sighed.

'Very well,' he said, 'if that's the way you want it.'

His hand shot out towards her, his long fingers closing over her arm.

Before she had a chance to utter another word, Jessica found herself standing on the carpet in front of him.

'Leave me alone,' she gasped, struggling to keep herself covered.

'Really, Jess,' he said, one brow raised, 'when are you going to stop this silly pretence? I'm your husband. Who do you think undressed you and put you to bed?'

She knew who'd undressed her, only too well, and her breath quickened. It wasn't something she liked to dwell on. So she set her face and simply refused to answer.

'You haven't changed much,' he went on, his voice smooth, reflective. 'A bit thinner, maybe, with all your ribs showing. But still, much the same.'

If she hadn't been certain that he was doing it on purpose, just to provoke her, Jessica might have seriously tried to kick his shins and chance the consequences, not that it would have done him much harm with her bare feet, but it would have made her feel a whole lot better. But somehow, she just about managed to stop herself, unwilling to give him the satisfaction, or the chance to retaliate.

Besides, she fumed, any show of fury and she might part company with the pyjama top altogether, and that was scarcely the effect she wanted!

'Please go,' she said again, and at long last, he complied.

'I've put some clothes out on the bed,' his parting shot came from the doorway.

'Thank you,' she said stiffly, 'but I can manage for myself. I'll be down as soon as I can,' she added pointedly.

For a minute or so, she waited, making quite sure he'd really gone, then Jessica made for the adjoining bathroom. A quick shower, a hasty grub dry with one of the thick, fluffy towels, and she was ready to get herself dressed. The clothes he'd chosen were lying on the bed, and grudgingly, she had to admit his choice couldn't be faulted. A pair of slim burgundy trousers, practical but supremely elegant, was exactly right for the chilly morning. Next to them lay a matching polo-neck top, together with a flowing overshirt of heavy ivory silk.

They were far prettier, far more feminine than the casual fleeces and jog bottoms she was used to now. Carefully, she brushed the soft folds with gentle fingertips, her eyes misting with bittersweet tears.

There had been a time when designer labels like these had been commonplace in her life. Hawke had never expected her to wear anything less. He was a generous man, she couldn't deny that, or he had been, she corrected herself stiffly. There wasn't much sign of generosity in his treatment of her now. Sighing, her hand reached out to take the beautiful garments, her conscience prodding uncomfortably. Should she give way, or stick to the clothes she'd tossed willy-nilly into her overnight case?

'Oh, put them on,' she said, femininity finally gaining the upper hand.

On the carpet stood a pair of boots in softest leather, to complete the outfit, and Jessica slipped them on. Her make-up was completed at the dressing-table, then she caught her long hair in a ribbon at the nape of her neck. Now, she was ready, even for Hawke. Smiling, she went over to lift the baby, and in a moment of true heart-lurching horror, realised he was gone.

Jessica had never moved so quickly, not in all her life. On terrified feet, she took the stairs two at a time, and when she finally reached the drawing room, she was panting and out of breath. Even then, she didn't pause. Fear spurred her on, and she flung herself bodily into the room. Hawke glanced up, his expression startled as she burst through the door. In one swift glance, she saw he was quite alone, lounging in a chair by the fire, reading a morning paper.

'Where's my baby?' she demanded, too far gone to bother with subtlety.

'Oh, Jess.'

He went back to his newspaper, exasperation deep in his voice.

'Hawke,' she insisted, simply refusing to be sidetracked, 'what have you done with him?'

Sighing, he put down his paper again, turning towards her.

'What do you think I've done with him?' he enquired coldly. 'Farmed him out to a poor shepherd family to bring up as their own, or left him out on the mountainside to die?'

'Don't be so silly,' she snapped.

'If you bother to look,' he added, his tone deeply sarcastic, 'you'll see that our son is safely asleep in his cot.'

He nodded towards the window, and there, fast asleep, was the baby, safely tucked up in a white creation trimmed lavishly with ribbon and lace. Jessica recognised it at once as the Munro family crib.

'Mother insisted on getting that out,' Hawke continued. 'After all, Gavin is my heir.'

Gavin! Heir! Jessica's thoughts danced an unearthly jig in her mind, making her head swim.

'What do you expect me to think?' she accused. 'You said you would take him away.'

'Only to Glen Marr, where he belongs, and didn't I give you the choice of coming, too?'

'Some choice,' she retorted, 'with you holding the baby!'

'That's more of a choice than you gave me,' he flashed back. 'If it had been left to you I would never have even set eyes on him.'

Jessica could find no words. How could she? She had never wanted to deprive him of his son, just keep him secret for a while, to protect herself until she was free. But would Hawke ever believe that?

'Have you nothing to say?' he demanded. 'Did I ever hurt you? What did I ever do to you that warranted losing my child?'

'It wasn't like that!'

The words were torn from her. She had to explain, make him understand.

'I just didn't want to be so tied.'

Even to her own ears, it sounded nonsense, a lame excuse, and she stumbled to silence.

'Didn't want to be tied?' he exclaimed, his eyes blazing. 'So what do you think marriage is? A game?'

'No, no,' she broke in.

She hadn't asked much, just a space to breathe, to grow, to be herself as well as Hawke's wife, but he wasn't prepared to listen to that.

'No more,' he rasped, 'but if you think I'm prepared to give up my son, now that I've found him, you couldn't be more wrong. So,'

51

he gritted, teeth clenched, his gaze raking her slender form, 'we have to put up with each other, whether we like it or not.'

He went back to his paper, the silence between them deafening, and Jessica drew in her breath. It was hard to compose herself, with her hands trembling, her heart beating like a drum. But gradually, her thoughts calmed, became less agitated, and she sank into the nearest chair.

'So be it,' she muttered to herself, 'but I'm not beaten yet, Hawke Munro. I'll do whatever it takes until I can get my son away.'

Jessica found Margaret in the smaller dining-room. The main banqueting hall, complete with beamed ceiling and carved minstrels' gallery, was only used for formal occasions, but the family room was still grander than anything she was used to now. Helping herself to cereal and toast from the sideboard, she joined her mother-in-law at the table, pouring herself a cup of piping hot coffee from the elegant Georgian pot. Margaret's eyes welcomed her, smiling over her gold-rimmed spectacles.

'It's lovely to have the family together again,' she said, 'and a new baby as well.'

For the life of her, Jessica couldn't reply to that. It was hardly lovely for her, but she managed a nod and a shaky smile. Hurting Margaret's feelings again so soon was something she wasn't looking forward to.

'He's asleep,' she finally said, side-stepping the subject, finding it was far easier to talk about the baby. 'Still in his cot,' she added, 'in the sitting room with Hawke.'

Margaret looked at her for a moment.

'I called my son Rufus,' she stated softly, 'so why don't you?'

Jessica shrugged, and with a valiant attempt at lightness, she smiled back.

'He calls himself Hawke,' she tried to explain. 'He always has to me.'

How could she say she thought the name suited him, down to the ground? The man was a hawk, a bird of prey, ruthless and determined to get his own way. He could never be Rufus to her.

'I like Rufus,' Margaret commented.

'And I liked Paul,' Jessica responded, the words out before she could stop them, 'but Hawke wants Gavin, so Gavin it has to be.'

'It was his grandfather's name.'

'And my father was called Paul.'

Outside, a few flakes of snow began to fall, fresh on the frozen drifts below, but most people would manage the short distance to the house. It seemed not even the weather dared to get in the way of Hawke's plans. The christening ceremony would go ahead. Jessica knew that now. If she tried to stop it, her wretched husband would probably hold it without her.

Margaret took her hand, holding it gently

between her two soft palms, her eyes on Jessica's pensive face.

'Smile, my dear,' she chided. 'Today is a happy day, remember.'

A happy day? Jessica wasn't too sure about that. It didn't seem particularly happy for her. Naturally enough, though, it was a quiet one, with only the family arriving for the ceremony, but that, at least, suited her mood. The quieter the better, so far as she was concerned.

Robert, the earl, tall and grey, dressed in his tartan, came up from the lodge he had made his home since his retirement, to hold the place of honour with Margaret by his side. He was delighted to see Jessica back, enveloping her in a warm hug.

'Glad to see you home,' he said. 'My son's been like a bear with a sore head without you around to keep him in line.'

'Really?' Jessica queried, and Hawke broke in at once, his expression brooding.

'No, not really,' he corrected sharply.

'That's your opinion,' his father replied. 'Ask anyone else, and you'll hear a different story.'

'A very different story,' Alastair, his brother, agreed with a grin. 'It's been misery up here.'

He was only a slightly smaller version of Hawke, but without all the enigmatic, hidden depths. An open man with a smiling, sun-weathered face, he grinned over at Jessica with unreserved pleasure.

'Rubbish!' Hawke insisted.

'See what I mean?' Alastair sighed, and shrugging in mock resignation, he added, 'I'm glad I don't have to live with him.'

Looking up, he caught the eye of his plump, gentle wife, busy ushering in their two little girls, and called her over. The girls, dressed in their best velvet dresses, one in green and one in red, took one look at Jessica and immediately began to wriggle, impatient to escape their mother's clutches.

'Ellie, Alice, leave poor Jessica alone,' Beth scolded, but Jessica shook her head.

She didn't mind their exuberant welcomes. She'd forgotten how much she'd missed them.

Strangely enough, no-one even mentioned her lost year. It seemed they were all too pleased to see her to ask any awkward questions. Either that, Jessica glowered inwardly, or what was far more likely, they had been warned off the subject by Hawke. Not that Jessica had much of a chance to find out, not with Hawke hovering at her side all the time. Chatting to anyone was simply out of the question, even if she'd felt like it. But by then, she was moving strictly on automatic pilot, her thoughts distracted, the word distant, unreal.

Miserably, she closed her eyes, her hands like ice at her sides. But when she opened them again, nothing had changed, and to make matters worse, everything on that whole dismal day seemed to be going Hawke's way. The baby behaved like an angel. He looked like one, too. Dressed in the flowing Munro baptism robe of ancient muslin and lace, he lay through the entire ceremony without a murmur, not even making a sound when the holy water was poured over his tiny head.

'I name this child Gavin Robert Paul,' the priest intoned, his voice resonating into the hushed silence, and Jessica caught her breath, a painful knot of unshed tears beginning to ache in her throat.

Jerkily, her hand rose to her mouth, trying to still her trembling lips. It was the moment she'd been dreading. The world had just turned upside down. Mercifully, the rest of the ceremony seemed to pass in a haze, her mind simply refusing to take it in. Afterwards, if she was asked, Jessica honestly couldn't recall a thing. Only the noise of the wind penetrated the fog in her mind, its melancholy voice beginning to rise again in the tall pines outside the manor windows.

She hated the very sound of it, moaning dolefully through the gathering twilight, but it wasn't entirely without its blessing. One swift look at the weather sent most of the guests scuttling for home. Only the immediate family stayed to drink the baby's health, for which small mercy Jessica offered up fervent prayers of thanks. Already, the start of a headache was beginning to throb behind her eyes, and her hand rose to her brow, trying to soothe away the pain.

'All right?' Hawke queried.

Dumbly, she nodded, though the walk back to the drawing-room had never seemed so long. But with Hawke's hand on her elbow, keeping her close, she managed to stay on her feet.

A huge log fire, blazing in the great stone hearth, welcomed them, and a christening cake, beribboned in satin and set on a silver salver, stood in state on the highly-polished table.

'Look,' one of the girls exclaimed, round-eyed, her gaze fixed on the snowy confection.

Even the sight of the child's excited face failed to lighten the weight, which had settled like stone around Jessica's heart. As they grouped around the fireplace, their glasses in their hands, only Margaret, her features glowing with joy, gave her any solace at all.

'Sit down. It's been a long day,' Hawke insisted, settling her into a chair by the fire, and she sank gratefully into its cushioned depths.

But his husbandly attentiveness, so charming on the surface, didn't fool her for a minute. Surreptitiously, she watched from beneath carefully lowered lashes, as he played the proud father. He hung over the crib, smiling, stroking his son's fluffy hair, examining his tiny hands between his own long fingers as if he couldn't quite believe they were real. To anyone else, she had to admit, it all looked very convincing.

'Something amiss, my dear?'

Jessica started, but she wasn't really surprised by the quiet voice interrupting her thoughts. To anyone with only half-an-eye, her face would have given her away, and like his son, no-one could ever accuse the earl of missing a thing. Observing her frown, he smiled towards her, one brow raised in a heart-lurching reminder of his oldest son. Slowly, he moved towards the fire, holding out his thin hands in front of the flames. He looked older, more frail, than when Jessica had last set eyes on him, but in spite of his years, he held himself erect.

'Well, my dear?' he queried again, and Jessica smiled back, shrugging her shoulders in what she hoped was a convincing display of lightness.

'Of course not,' she said.

'She's just tired,' Hawke put in, leaving the crib at once and coming over to Jessica's side. 'It was a long journey here,' he added, 'and today has been a long day. It's been too much all at once.'

For a moment, his father's eyes flicked over him, their expression veiled, then he shrugged and turned away. It was a credible explanation, even to Jessica's ears, and she couldn't blame the earl for accepting it. In his place, she would have probably done the same.

'I'm sure everything's fine,' Margaret said, 'but Rufus is right. It's been a tiring day, and now it's time for us all to go home.'

Beth sent her daughters running to fetch their coats, and Alastair finished his drink hurriedly. But Jessica froze solid. Please, she pleaded, don't leave me alone with Hawke!

'Aren't you staying tonight?' she blurted out, her eyes wide, fixed on Margaret's face.

'You don't need me any longer,' Margaret replied and she allowed her husband to help her into her coat.

'Do you think you'll get home, in all this snow?' Jessica persisted, but the earl nodded encouragingly, patting her arm.

'Don't worry,' he comforted softly. 'Alastair has the Land-Rover. He'll drop us off at the lodge on his way home. Margaret will be quite safe.'

Alastair nodded, and he started to gather his daughters together.

'Come on, girls,' he insisted briskly. 'Let's take Grandma and Grandpa home before it gets too late.'

'Well, if you're sure,' Jessica finally conceded, forcing a steadiness into her voice she was far from feeling.

It nearly killed her to smile, but somehow, from somewhere, she managed a fairly credible imitation as the party made for the door.

'See you soon,' Margaret called from the

car, and Jessica nodded.

She couldn't reply, not aloud. She didn't dare trust herself to speak. It was one thing to try to look unconcerned with everyone watching, but quite another to keep it up after they were gone. The iron grip she had on her feelings vanished abruptly with the departing car, and Jessica fled back inside, leaving Hawke standing alone on the doorstep.

The drawing-room was warm after the freezing evening outside. Too warm for comfort, and with trembling hands, she helped herself to another glass of champagne. It might help, she reflected faintly, might bring her some sort of oblivion, anything rather than just sitting there, trying to pretend nothing was wrong, when actually, nothing was right.

Close behind her, she heard Hawke come into the room, his footsteps firm on the polished floor, but she made no attempt to break the silence. Staring hard into the fire, she sipped her wine, still hoping forlornly for some delayed, soothing effect, but her mind only seemed to get sharper, her position clearer and more precise.

She was alone for the night with Hawke, with the man who still considered himself her husband, and all the champagne in the world couldn't change that.

CHAPTER FOUR

The silence grew deeper, lingering unbearably between them, pressing down like a physical weight, but neither attempted to speak. The clink of a glass, the sound of pouring liquid indicated Hawke was helping himself to a brandy from the decanter on the sideboard, and swiftly, Jessica threw him a sideways look. She wanted to know what he was up to.

He was doing exactly what she'd expected, standing with his back to her, still formally dressed in an impeccable dark grey suit, his attention firmly on his drink. From where she was sitting, she could see his tie was loose, his jacket open, and even as she watched, he pulled the tie over his head. Carelessly, he threw it over the back of the nearest chair and undid the top two buttons of his shirt.

Half-hoping she could take the baby and get upstairs, if only she was quiet enough, she began to get up from her chair. Then he turned, quickly, and caught her watching him.

'Want to join me, Mrs Munro?' he asked, lifting his glass in mock salute.

'Don't call me that,' she snapped, immediately on the alert.

'Why not?' he returned smoothly. 'It's your name, isn't it?'

'Not anymore, not really,' she tried to insist,

her voice deceptively firm, but he only smiled, deep into her eyes.

'Oh, but it is,' he murmured.

His voice resonated in her ears, its tone like silk but just as insistent as hers, and Jessica sat very still. Suddenly, the room was electric. Hawke meant trouble. Jessica knew it. She could see it, hear it, feel it, in his narrowed eyes, in the seductive, whispering voice. Hastily, she leaped to her feet, a tremor of unease feathering along her spine.

'I'll take the baby upstairs,' she said, her eyes very carefully turned away.

A sober Hawke she could deal with, but a Hawke even slightly influenced by drink was quite another matter.

'But it's not nine o'clock,' he queried incredulously.

'It's been a long day, you said so yourself,' she flashed back.

With a studied attempt at calm, she rose to her feet and made her way towards the crib. Unhurriedly, she lifted the baby, but Hawke had moved to stand between her and the door.

'I said, not yet,' he drawled softly.

Obviously, he wasn't in any mood for listening, not to her, not to anyone. Every inch of his huge frame oozed power and determination, a ruthless combination when it was aroused, but Jessica wasn't without commonsense. She gave him one look upwards, meeting those compelling eyes, and decided to concede to the inevitable. Crossing him now was pointless. It would only push things completely beyond her control.

'You want to talk?' she queried, and nodding assent, she seated herself again in the chair by the fire, their son in her arms. Somehow, she had to inject some sanity into the situation. 'Go on, then,' she invited.

Abruptly, he turned, pacing back to the sideboard.

'Who said I wanted to talk?' he demanded, pouring himself another brandy.

'It's all that's on offer,' she returned evenly.

He laughed, softly, with a faint, cynical amusement, the sound making the hairs on the back of her neck stand finely on end, and he took an easy step towards her.

'You haven't always said that,' he reminded, eyes hooded, fire burning in their depths.

Colour flamed her cheeks, but she returned his gaze look for look. Determination not to give way kept her head held high.

'Things are different now,' she insisted.

'They needn't be.'

'Yes, they do,' she replied, managing to keep her features surprisingly composed under that watchful look.

Outwardly calm, she got to her feet, ignoring the nervous somersaults her poor stomach was making.

'If you've nothing more sensible to say,' she added, 'I think I will go upstairs after all.'

'Sit down,' he insisted softly. 'You're quite safe. I don't make a habit of forcing myself on women, even those I happen to have married.'

'Then behave yourself,' she parried, and with a shrug, he placed his glass back on the sideboard.

'You drive a hard bargain,' he commented softly.

'I don't drive bargains at all.'

Her answer was immediate, short and unequivocal, and his eyes narrowed.

'You're telling me,' he replied with feeling. 'No discussions from you, no bargains. Just take off without a word.'

'Oh, Hawke,' she sighed. 'It wasn't without a word. We agreed.'

'To a temporary separation, a breathing space, not to a divorce.'

It was the answer she was expecting, of course, but hearing the words, spoken aloud in that unmistakable tone, drove all the blood from her face. Wide-eyed and pale, she took a deep breath, then another, her hands clenching and unclenching at her sides, but she made herself meet his eyes.

'Why not?' she queried. 'We married too soon.'

'Then we repent at leisure.'

His answer was rough, the tone harsh. Brusquely, he turned back to this drink, refilling his glass and tossing down the amber liquid with one swift swallow.

'No,' she snapped. 'Just look at you, Hawke. As soon as I don't say what you want to hear, you dismiss it, ignore it, go back to your drinking.'

'Don't try to accuse me of alcoholism now.'

'No, no. I didn't mean that.'

She didn't. Drinking too much had never been a failing of his, unless it was something he had fallen into since she'd been away.

'At least,' she stammered, 'I don't think I do.'

'Oh, don't worry,' he repeated, replacing his glass with exaggerated care on the sideboard. 'But what do you expect me to think? You went away, hiding the fact you were carrying my child.'

'I didn't!'

'Of course you did,' he cut in at once. 'Gavin is almost two months old. You left here in the summer. Even I can add up the months.'

Sadly, she sighed, her eyes misting with sudden tears, and Hawke faltered to a close, his eyes darkening a fraction.

'He was premature,' she whispered. 'He came too soon, but he was always strong, like you. He was never in any real danger.'

'And you?'

Dismissively, she shrugged, her expression veiled, her eyes taking on a shuttered look as she carefully rearranged her son in her arms.

'I'm OK,' she prevaricated, shrugging aside his question. 'I survived, and I want a divorce,' she added firmly. 'What do you want, Hawke?'

There, it was out in the open, the question she'd been dying to ask. She glanced sideways, into his face. Would he say he wanted his family together? But with a shrug of those broad shoulders, he merely took a seat in the chair opposite, stretching out his long legs in front of the blaze.

'I want my son,' he stated smoothly.

He'd made no mention of her, and Jessica's stomach lurched wildly, then settled none too steadily somewhere in the region of her boots. She thanked heaven she was sitting down, or the shock might have felled her flat at his feet. Carefully, she stiffened her spine, her arms tightening about her child. It wasn't easy, trying to look unconcerned under that direct, disconcerting gaze. Regarding her closely, his sculptured features set like iron, he emanated an air of authority that turned her bones to water.

He looked so sure of himself, wearing his mantle of self-assurance as easily as a second skin. This was a man born of power and respect, and if that wasn't enough, he was a successful businessman into the bargain, well versed in the art of giving orders, taking decisions. Impinging on the lives of hundreds was an everyday fact of life to him. Against such a lethal adversary, what earthly chance would she have? But pride finally came to her aid. This was her son, too, they were discussing. If Hawke thought for one second he could just wave her aside, he could think again. She gazed back at him, her eyes just as unflinching.

'So do I,' she started clearly.

He looked somewhat taken aback by the firm little voice, the resolution in her expression, and imperceptibly, his mouth hardened. But he merely nodded, his gaze holding a degree of brooding respect.

'Of course,' he allowed, 'so we need to talk.'

'Yes,' she agreed, 'but that means listening as well, on both sides,' she added, accentuating the words with cold insistence. 'You, too. No power games, no bullying.'

'I didn't think you intended to bully me,' his voice cut in. 'Have I something to fear?'

Just for a moment, for the merest space of a heartbeat, she could have sworn she heard a faint, teasing note in his tone, like the old Hawke, the Hawke from before. In those days, she would have leaped across, grinning, to sit in his lap, kissing him firmly into silence until they'd ended up in each other's arms.

Swiftly, she glanced upwards, meeting those compelling eyes. But she could see nothing there, no amusement, no recognition of the love they'd once shared, and a cold, hollow feeling settled around her heart. It was only her imagination, playing its cruel tricks. Glen Marr, with all its bittersweet, half-buried memories, had reached out to ensnare her, and she had almost dropped her guard.

Her body quivered. The wave of desolation was sudden, chilling, the disappointment sharp, taking her by surprise. Hastily, she bent her head, chewing miserably on her bottom lip to try to stop it from trembling. But she wasn't quite quick enough. Hawke obviously saw the distress in her face before she managed to vanquish it.

'You look tired,' he broke in, his voice softer, less commanding. 'Perhaps we should sleep on it, talk in the morning.'

'I would prefer that,' she admitted quietly, and in spite of herself, she threw him a grateful look.

'Good,' he said, rising to his feet. 'We'll both be more clear headed after a good night's sleep. So, until then.'

He inclined his head, briefly, and made for the door. Almost in disbelief, Jessica watched him go, heard his steps fading along the hall, and in her mind's eye she saw him going into his study, closing the door, leaving her in peace. It was a minor miracle, almost a victory, and her heart quickened its beat. With the first real smile on her face for weeks, she almost danced the last few steps to the foot of the stairs. Round one was definitely over. Now she had to prepare for round two.

The following day dawned clear and still with scarcely a breath of air stirring the trees outside. It was crisp and cold, but happily, the sky was blue and even the sun was trying to put in an appearance.

The grandfather clock in the hall was striking nine o'clock as Jessica made her way down the sweep of staircase, the baby in her arms. He settled so peacefully in his crib in the drawing-room, she had not worried about leaving him to get her own breakfast. But surprisingly, the dining-room door was closed. As she approached, she heard the sound of voices coming from inside. Hawke, it definitely was, and a woman. Margaret? She smiled hopefully.

At once, she threw open the door, then the smile of welcome froze on her lips. Sitting with Hawke at the table wasn't Margaret at all, but one of the most beautiful women Jessica had ever set eyes on.

'Hello,' she stammered.

'Ah, Jess,' Hawke said easily, 'this is Moira Arriannos, a very old friend of mine.'

'Not so much of the old,' his companion corrected sweetly.

Tall and willowy slim, her make-up and clothes would have done credit to a model straight out of the latest glossy fashion magazine. She made Jessica feel skinny and awkward, hovering in the doorway, unsure of her welcome. Involuntarily, she swallowed hard. Stop that right now, she scolded herself. You're behaving like a child.

Pulling herself together, swiftly, Jessica

69

composed her face. Lightly, she took a step into the room, a welcoming smile fixed to her lips.

'How nice to meet you, Mrs Arriannos,' she nodded, her tone as sweet as honey itself. 'I'm Jessica Munro, Hawke's wife.'

Moira Arriannos's beautifully-shaped brows rose, and she threw Jessica a questioning look. Leaning forward to show off her classical profile, like the ivory head on a cameo brooch, Jessica was sure she knew what a striking picture she made.

'How nice,' she purred. 'The loving wife.'

'Of course,' Jessica agreed, her tone dry, but although Hawke threw her a slanting look, his eyes narrowed, Moira evidently missing the slightly mocking inflection.

'How lovely,' she continued unabashed, 'and with a baby as well.'

She turned her attention back to Hawke. Jessica had to smother a smile, hurriedly lifting a slender hand to her lips. It seemed Moira was the kind of woman who needed a man in her world, a man to lean on, to play the helpless woman for.

'It was awful,' she was saying, her voice low and breathy, 'with my car stuck in the snow. I don't know what I would have done if you hadn't been around.'

The comment wasn't addressed to her, so Jessica didn't need to answer. Silently, she helped herself to breakfast and took a seat opposite. It was even easy to look sympathetic, as the flow of stories were directed mainly at Hawke. All Jessica needed to do was nod and look interested, and that wasn't too difficult if she kept her attention mainly on her food, until Moira suddenly rose dramatically from her chair.

'I'm very tired,' she murmured, one slim hand raised to her head. 'I think I need to lie down.'

Hawke leaped immediately to his feet.

'I'll show you to your room,' he insisted at once.

Moira hung on to his arm, swaying against him rather more closely than was strictly necessary, Jessica noted sourly. The woman's dark mane of hair feathering around her face like chrysanthemum petals was actually touching Hawke's shoulder, tall as he was, while Jessica herself could have easily walked beneath her husband's outstretched arms.

'She's had a bad time,' he threw out in brief explanation, lifting an arm to support Moira's elegant shoulders. 'Her car was trapped in a drift, and she had to walk here.'

'It took me hours,' his companion breathed, milking the scene for every tiny vestige of effect. 'I was so frightened, so cold.'

Jessica forced a concerned smile to her face, but to her, the whole thing rang supremely false, posed, like a scene from a play, and not a very good play, at that. Again, she struggled to hide behind a set of polite features. Surely no-one would ever be taken in by such an obvious charade. No woman could be that helpless, but Hawke's eyes held no hint of disbelief. He was smiling, deep into Moira's upturned grey eyes, totally taken in.

'Don't mind me,' Jessica commented.

They didn't. With another brief apology, tossed over his shoulder almost as an afterthought, Hawke ushered Moira from the room, leaving Jessica sitting at the table, alone. For what seemed like an age, she didn't move, scarcely taking a breath, trying to tell herself she didn't care. Surely, she reasoned, this was the answer to all her prayers. A liaison with another woman would get Hawke out of her hair for good.

So why didn't she feel better about it? Rigidly, she held herself erect, a whole gamut of emotions running deep in her soul. Resentment gripped her, together with more than a twinge of fear and a slow, deep, teeth-gritting indignation. But there wasn't one tiny shred of relief. Her hands clenched into angry, little fists in her lap. For the first time in her life, she knew what it was like to wish another human being real physical harm. She could have happily killed Moira Arriannos.

'You're jealous.'

With a tiny start, Jessica realised it was her own voice she could hear, soft and shaky, whispered into the breathless silence.

Miserably, she shook her head, a sense of disbelief washing through her, hating the cold knot of pain suddenly blocking her throat. Jealous, of Moira? It couldn't be true.

Wretchedly, Jessica's hand lifted, and trembling fingers brushed the slender curve of her throat, trying to ease away the ache. Oh, of course it was true—she still loved Hawke! That was the trouble. She had always loved Hawke. It was living with him she found the problem. She was his wife, and nothing on earth was too good for her. He would cherish her, protect her, indulge her every whim, then simply refuse to countenance her slightest desire for independence. But judging by this morning's performance, Moira was different. She didn't mind playing the sweet, little helpless woman one tiny bit. To her, it came as naturally as breathing.

Numbly, Jessica finished her breakfast, going through the motions like a robot. The toast seemed to have turned to ashes in her mouth and even the freshly-ground coffee had lost its flavour, but it didn't matter. Nothing matters now. Coming back to Glen Marr had done its worst. She just couldn't live in this house, sleep in their bed, and not remember how much she loved her husband. In London, she could harden her heart against him. At Glen Marr, she knew she hadn't a chance.

The room vanished momentarily behind a shimmering mist of tears, and she blinked

73

them away. How could she have been so blind? It had never been Hawke she couldn't trust. It was her own treacherous feelings for him.

'Madam?'

Helen, the young maid, came into the room, and hovered in the doorway, a questioning look on her young face.

'What is it?' Jessica asked softly.

'May I clear away now? Mrs Ogilvie would like to see you in the library just now, and I wonder if you'd finished.'

With a nod, Jessica got up from her place at the table and allowed the girl to get on with her work. She hadn't the faintest idea why the housekeeper wanted to see her, but before searching the woman out in the library, she went back to the drawing-room to check on Gavin in his cot.

He wasn't alone. Hawke was lounging in his chair by the side of the fire, his head buried again in his paper. He didn't even glance up, and illogically, Jessica's blood pressure shot up a notch or two. How dare he sit there so much at his ease, ignoring her, when he'd just brought that hateful woman into their house!

'Well?' she demanded through gritted teeth.

He looked up then, a startled expression flitting across his handsome features, and his eyebrows rose at the sight of her flushed face.

'What is it now?' he queried.

'Don't play the innocent with me,' she shot back. 'Who is this woman?'

She tossed the words at him, her voice dropping scorn, as if it was the highest insult she could possibly utter.

'Moira?' he enquired incredulously.

His expression remained polite, regarding her rigid figure slightly askance. He was definitely looking down his nose at her, and just the sight of him sent all caution flying to the winds.

'Who else?' she snapped. 'Unless you've a dozen other women secreted about the place.'

'I haven't any women secreted about the place, as you so politely put it. Moira is an old friend.'

'Just a friend?'

She didn't believe him, not for a moment, and it showed rather too clearly in her face.

'We were friends,' he broke in, sighing, 'as children. We grew up together. That's all. Maybe,' he added, spreading his hands, 'when we were younger, much younger, our parents, or friends, thought we might marry.'

'Marry?' her voice emerged as no more than a squeak. 'What do you mean, marry?'

'Marry?' his voice queried, a calm drawl as he shrugged those great shoulders. 'I think it meant much the same then as it does now.'

His offhand tone, the raised brows, only added to her anger, and she gritted her teeth, her eyes blazing like dark jewels. But before she had a chance to toss out another word, he interrupted again.

'Before you ask,' he stated smoothly, 'she left to marry a very wealthy shipping magnate, a Greek, who whisked her off to a villa in Crete. Glen Marr didn't stand a chance.'

'And now?'

'Now.' He shrugged. 'She's a very wealthy widow.'

Her eyes widened in shocked disbelief. So that was it! Hawke's lost love, returned to him after all these years! No wonder he'd hung on the woman's every word. He must be hoping this was his second chance.

'Who might come back here,' she ground out, finishing for him.

'Hopefully,' he agreed.

Her eyes flew to his face, fixing there, sparkling with unsuppressed indignation, and the lazy amusement on his dark features did nothing at all to settle her temper.

'Why not?' he repeated. 'This her home, after all. Why shouldn't she come back? It won't matter to you, if you want a divorce.'

Just in time, Jessica managed to close her mouth. The words she wanted to throw at him caught on her lips. Take a deep breath, she urged herself, and for goodness' sake, try to think what you're saying.

'True,' she acknowledged, nodding, with a belated attempt at reason, 'but we have Gavin to think of now. If you want to share custody of our son, I have to be sure of the company you keep.'

She hadn't meant the remark to be quite so insulting, but it came out sounding just that. Silently, he rose from his chair, crossing the room to stand within touching distance, and she drew in a shuddery breath, every fine hair on her skin standing acutely on end at his closeness.

'And what precisely do you mean by that?' he queried.

There wasn't a single thing she could say. She didn't know what she meant herself, let alone to explain it to him. Numbly, she tried to move away, putting a safe distance between them, but he followed her.

'Well?' he demanded.

She was saved by the bell, or rather, by a soft knock on the door. The sound of it pulled him up short.

'Come in,' Jessica called at once, not taking any chances, and with a shrug, Hawke went back to his chair by the fire.

It was Mrs Ogilvie, a smile on her round face, and as she came into the room, her eyes searched out Jessica.

'There you are, madam,' she said. 'I've been waiting to see you since breakfast.'

It seemed, since she was back, Mrs Ogilvie fully expected Jessica to see to the running of the house again, so for the next hour or so, Jessica found herself caught up in detailed domestic discussions with the housekeeper. They went through everything, even down to what time she wanted the fires lit, but she drew the line at appointing a nursery nurse for the new little master, as the housekeeper referred to Gavin.

'I can look after him myself,' she broke in.

'Very well, madam, if you insist.'

'I do. Now, is there anything else?'

There wasn't anything she could think of, so the housekeeper took herself back to her work. But by then, Gavin was stirring in his cot, ready for another feed. Jessica picked him up, holding the tiny body close as she carried him upstairs, and the gong was actually sounding for lunch before she was free again.

To her surprise, Moira Arriannos was sitting alone in the dining-room, a lost expression on her lovely features. She looked up at once and smiled, fixing large grey eyes on Jessica's face.

'Oh, hello again,' she said. 'I thought I was going to be by myself, with no-one to talk to.'

Her tone was so pathetic Jessica felt almost sorry for the woman. She'd obviously been indulged in the past, the centre of all attention, and she expected the same from everyone.

'I thought you were resting,' Jessica excused herself, and turning her attention away from Moira's self-pitying face, she helped herself to soup from the hostess trolley.

'Oh, dear,' Moira broke in, her voice a comical squeak of dismay, 'do we have to wait on ourselves?'

'We do, at family, mealtimes,' Jessica

affirmed.

She was fighting to keep the note of incredulity out of her voice. The woman really was helpless. Helpless or hopeless, she couldn't be sure.

'The servants cook the food and bring it here,' she added quietly, 'but we usually manage to help ourselves.'

When she realised Jessica wasn't joking, Moira got to her feet with a long-suffering sigh and made her way to the trolley.

'I suppose I'd better get used to this,' she said with a sigh, 'now I'm back in Glen Marr.'

Jessica stared at her, the breath stopped in her throat. Even her heart seemed to take on a slower beat. Was this really the answer to all her prayers? Somehow, she couldn't believe it.

'For good?' she forced out at last.

'Oh, yes,' came Moira's immediate reply. 'I'm coming home, and dear Hawke says he'll help me settle in again. Isn't that lovely?'

CHAPTER FIVE

At that precise moment, dear Hawke himself chose to appear in the doorway, as if on cue, and Moira's smile flashed out at once to welcome him. She turned her pale, wide eyes over towards him, lashes fluttering, slanting him a glowing look.

'Hello,' she purred. 'I've missed you. Were you busy?'

'I went over to see Father.'

He shrugged, helping himself to a plateful of food and bringing it to the table.

'I thought he'd be tired, after yesterday. He's used to a quiet life now.'

'He's OK?' Jessica queried swiftly.

Anxiously, she threw her husband a worried glance. She knew the earl had a heart complaint, a mild one, which worried his wife and sons far more than it worried him. It was the reason, though, that Margaret had moved them into the lodge the moment he had retired. It was smaller, less of an effort to get around, she'd insisted, and when Margaret made up her mind, her family knew better than to try to dissuade her, so the young people had taken the house, Hawke and his bride.

'He's just a little tired, resting after yesterday,' Hawke nodded, answering the query, his calm voice chasing the bittersweet images from Jessica's head. 'But he should be all right.'

'Then we could have been chatting, catching up with old times.'

Moira pouted, and Jessica clenched her hands into small, tight fists in her lap, feeling her irritation beginning to rise. There wasn't much doubt where the woman's real interests lay, and it certainly wasn't with her, or with the old earl's state of health, for that matter.

'I thought you were resting,' Jessica put in pointedly, 'after your ordeal.'

Moira tore her gaze away from Hawke's face, her eyes flicking over Jessica's stiffened form for all the world as if she'd only just realised anyone else was present.

'I was,' she agreed, her tone plaintive in the extreme, 'but I was feeling so lonely, all by myself in my room.'

'And we can't have that,' Hawke broke in easily. 'We must take care of our guests, mustn't we, Jess?'

'Absolutely,' Jessica hissed, her eyes frosty.

The woman really was childish, she fumed. Surely Hawke could see that. Any minute now he would laugh or shrug, his eyes mocking, but he didn't do either, and in the silence that followed, Jessica took up her spoon again, fixing her attention firmly back on her soup. Somehow, though, it seemed to have lost its taste, and she pushed it away.

81

'Don't you like it?' Hawke queried, brows raised in an expression of exaggerated concern. 'Never mind, I'll get you something else.'

He rose, before she had a chance to protest, and went back to the trolley. He cut her a generous slice of cheese-and-herb flan, whistling softly to himself as he added salad and a helping of tiny, new potatoes.

'I can't eat all that,' Jessica gasped in dismay, as he placed it on the table before her.

'Sure you can,' he insisted, throwing her a glittering smile. 'You're skin and bone, and you have a baby to feed as well, remember?'

As if she could ever forget that! If she didn't have a baby, his baby, she wouldn't be there at all. She picked up a knife and fork, ready to tackle the meal in front of her. It wasn't worth arguing about, she decided stiffly, at least, not here, in front of Moira.

'Well, I'm hungry, terribly hungry,' the other woman simpered. 'Will you get me something, darling, but not so much of that pie thing? I have my figure to think of.'

Surprisingly, Hawke did as he was asked at once. Rising to his feet, he nodded, but he heaped Moira's plate equally as full as Jessica's and Jessica had to hide a smile at the look on that lovely face.

'Eat up,' he said and smiled. 'It's all good, organic, home-produced food.'

'But my waistline,' Moira whispered.

'It will always be beautiful,' Hawke returned, his voice soft. 'Besides, I like a woman with a few curves.'

The words were light, but they had a taunting edge to them that Jessica was sure she wasn't intended to miss. Boy, but the man had gall, flirting with Moira in front of her very eyes, comparing their figures and finding hers lacking. Instinctively, she felt her hackles rise. Wretch, she reflected sourly, but she held her tongue. She wouldn't give him the satisfaction of a reply. Instead, she smiled sweetly and began to demolish the food on her plate.

'You're right,' she agreed, after a couple of forkfuls, 'this is good.'

Hawke threw her a swift, sideways glance, his eyes intent.

'Of course,' he returned. 'Aren't I always right?'

'I know you always think you are.'

A muscle twitched in Hawke's jaw but, tight-mouthed, he refrained from comment, and Jessica smothered a smile. It was a heady feeling, having the last word. It didn't happen that often with her self-assured husband, and her lashes fluttered downwards to cover the faint sparkle of triumph glinting in the dark depths of her eyes.

After that, the meal took on a somewhat unreal air, with Moira's voice prattling on and on, mercifully aimed mainly at Hawke, giving Jessica a chance to sit back and draw breath.

83

Observing their guest with incredulous eyes, she found herself wondering if the woman was actually quite clever, manipulating the situation to suit herself. But after listening to the girlish tinkle of laughter for the umpteenth time, to the shamelessly coy conversation, she was convinced Moira really was as empty-headed as she appeared.

'I think I'll leave you now,' she excused herself at last, rising from the table, but to her exasperation, Hawke rose, too.

'We'll join you,' he stated easily. 'I'll ring for Helen. She can bring the coffee into the drawing-room.'

It was the last thing on earth Jessica wanted, the enforced company of Hawke and his silly girlfriend. She didn't think she could bear the sound of that chattering voice for very much longer. But what could she do? Wordlessly, she retraced her steps, all thoughts of escaping to the relative safety of her own room vanishing into thin air like smoke, and with gritted teeth, she sank into the nearest chair. There was nothing else for it. She had to smile and play hostess in Hawke's maddening little game.

The rest of the afternoon descended rapidly into a farce, though for the life of her, Jessica couldn't quite grasp the funny side of it all. Even the baby slept like a log, giving her no excuse to get away, and she was trapped in her chair, sipping politely at her coffee. Surreptitiously, she glanced towards the ornate old clock ticking away on the mantelpiece, but to her horror, its hands insisted it was only ten minutes past two.

It wasn't possible, she groaned inwardly. She could have sworn it was later than that. It seemed later, much later, but time wasn't on her side. It was going its own way, dragging on and on and she was forced to sit, smiling brightly until her face positively ached, trying to make some kind of sensible conversation.

It wasn't the easiest thing in the world to do, not with Moira so intent on charming her husband in front of her very eyes. Gritting her teeth, she watched as the woman went into what had to be one of the best performances of her life.

'Shall I get you a drink?' Moira simpered, leaning towards Hawke's tall figure with a coy smile on her lovely face, and when he nodded, she swayed over to the sideboard, smoothing the silky material of her blouse over her curvy form.

'Anything for you,' she purred, fluttering her silver-tipped lashes provocatively in his direction, and Jessica felt distinctly sick to the stomach.

Moira was pouring the wine with many a captivating glance in Hawke's direction. Evidently the woman could wait on Hawke, she noted uncharitably, only waiting on herself was beneath her dignity.

'There,' Moira simpered, sitting down

again, as close to him as she could decently get, 'a drink for the man of the house.'

Jessica watched in sheer disbelief as Hawke took the offered glass. But the wretched man seemed mesmerised. He lounged back into his seat entirely at his ease, the silliest grin on his face. Stiffening her back, she tried to tell herself she didn't care. Why should she? It was a divorce she wanted, and if Hawke decided to tie himself to the empty-headed Moira, that was his look-out, not hers.

'Are you hoping to stay in Glen Marr for long?' she finally broke in, with a belated attempt at steering the conversation away from the mutual admiration society going on under her nose.

'Oh, dear,' Moira whispered dramatically, turning large, sad eyes towards her, 'am I in the way already?'

Jessica bit her tongue, sharply, sorely tempted to blurt out the truth. The words were tantalisingly close, hovering on her lips, but somehow she managed to choke them back. Good manners forbade her to be so rude to Hawke's guest.

'Of course you're not in the way,' Hawke put in quickly, his face dark with displeasure. 'Whatever made you think that?'

His glance towards Jessica was icy, intended to freeze her to the bone. At the very least, it was meant to stop any further remarks dead in their tracks. But even his answer, swiftly as it came, wasn't enough to mollify Moira. She drooped, hand to eyes, in a show of sorrowful tears.

'You're so kind,' she sobbed, 'but I can see it's not a convenient time for me to be here, not for Jessica, anyway.'

In the silence that followed, Jessica raised a hand to brush a stray tendril of hair from her face, her dark eyes stormy. Good manners or not, she couldn't leap in with the invitation Moira was angling for. The words would choke her. Angrily, she bit her lip as Hawke broke in and did it for her.

'Rubbish,' he insisted, and he patted Moira's shoulder with a powerful hand. 'You can stay as long as you like, can't she, Jess?'

What could Jessica say? Anything but agreement would only look churlish, ungracious, maybe hint of jealousy. Heaven forbid that, she breathed, her head thrown up high. Besides, this was Hawke's house. He could have whomsoever he liked there.

'Of course,' she concurred, lifting her slender shoulders in a small, dismissive shrug, 'whatever you say.'

'That's settled then,' Hawke stated, his eyes fixed on Moira's face. 'You're welcome here for as long as you like.'

At once, the tremulous mouth ceased its drooping, and Moira brushed the tears from her lashes with a slender hand.

'If you're sure I'm no trouble,' she

whispered.

The grey eyes rested on Hawke's dark features, the face upturned towards him, its expression almost beseeching, inviting his reassurance.

Good grief, Jessica almost exploded out loud, this is more than flesh and blood can stand. Hastily, she rose to her feet. If she didn't get away soon, she feared she might be physically sick.

'I think I'll take the baby upstairs,' she announced quickly. 'He must be almost ready for a feed.'

She was right. He was more than ready, and she sank into the chair upstairs, settling him gently against her. She still couldn't believe that Moira could be so saccharine sweet, so coy, not truly, not in this day and age.

'Though your daddy seems to like it well enough,' she muttered grimly against her son's soft, fluffy head.

Outside the window, the sun was fading fast, filling the room with shadows, and she sighed under her breath. She was still in love with Hawke. He was her husband, her lover, the father of her child, and he was turning to another woman right in front of her eyes.

'But I can't be like her,' she sighed to the sleepy infant. 'That was the problem. I never could.'

For a very long time she sat, holding her baby, her eyes gazing sightlessly into space.

Only the sound of Hawke's voice from the doorway finally brought her back to the world.

'Are you coming down for dinner?' he asked, and she turned dull eyes towards him.

'I'm still awfully tired,' she excused herself.

'Very well.' He shrugged. 'I'm sure I can keep Moira amused.'

I'm sure you can, Jessica breathed to herself as he closed the door. He could hardly wait to get back to her. Sighing, she settled the baby in his crib, and she went into the bathroom to splash cold water on to her wrists and temples. Maybe that would make her feel better. She certainly needed something. Later, Helen brought her a dinner tray. Jessica made a valiant attempt on the plateful of pasta, and when the young maid removed what was left of the meal, she decided to take an early night.

After stripping off her clothes, she took a swift bath, and ignoring the robe lying over the back of a chair, she wrapped herself in a towel and padded back into the bedroom. The huge bed looked soft and immensely inviting. Suddenly, all she wanted to do was bury herself under the quilt and sleep, and she started to rub herself dry, when a knock on the door made her start like a frightened deer.

'Yes?' she queried, just a little warily.

'It's only me,' the familiar voice called out, a heart-stoppingly familiar voice, and her heart seemed to kick abruptly into overdrive.

She didn't want Hawke of all people

89

walking in on her now. She had to keep him at arm's length. If she didn't, heaven knows what would happen. But before she could reply, he turned the handle and opened the door.

'What do you want?' she snapped, with just a little more heat than she really intended.

It made not one jot of difference. He stood his ground, not in the least put out. His eyes roamed over her, from top to toe, a narrowed half-smile playing on his lips as if he found her mildly amusing.

'It's getting late,' she added quickly, with as much force as she could manage, 'and I for one am ready for bed.'

Instantly, the hot colour leaped into her face. She'd said the wrong thing, she knew it at once. She could see it in his sudden smile, the speculative, gleaming eyes.

'So am I,' he murmured, in a voice as soft and smooth as silk.

She wanted to run, get away, fast, forgetting any idea of decorum, throwing all dignity to the winds, but there was nowhere to go. She was transfixed, her eyes enormous, her skin flushed wildly to rose.

Coolly, Hawke gazed down at her, his look deep and compelling, holding her frozen to the spot.

'Don't fool yourself,' she flashed back, her tone angry, disdainful. 'I'm not issuing any invitations.'

'No?' he queried, looking her over.

He appeared so self-assured, arrogant even, she could have screamed. The man just wouldn't be put down!

'No,' she assured him icily.

His eyes roamed over her, easily, at will, finally coming to rest on her upturned face, their expression so deeply aware that she was powerless to prevent a warm, tinge of colour rising again in her cheeks. But she held up her head to meet his gaze.

'I'd almost forgotten how delightful you are,' he said, 'if a trifle sour at the centre.'

Sour? Had he really said sour? This time, anger flared through her, lifting her chin, lending a diamond brightness to her eyes. But grimly, she held it in check.

'Shall I dry your back?' he drawled on, and her body heat rose abruptly as he pushed his way through the doorway, closing the door behind him.

'No, thank you,' she snapped, though her voice held a quiver she couldn't quite manage to hide.

'You're sure?' he persisted, and swiftly, she nodded her head.

'I'm sure.'

The cheek of the man, thinking he could roll up at her door at bedtime, expecting to be invited in! She longed to tell him what he could do with himself, and in no uncertain terms at that, but her voice seemed stuck in her throat. It didn't help much to think that

Moira might hear, either. So grimly, Jessica shook her head, resolutely holding her tongue.

Hawke was still smiling down at her, his mouth an enigmatic curve, his eyes resting openly on her face. Gently, he reached out, firmly lifting her chin.

'Hawke,' she protested stiffly.

'Yes?' he returned serenely.

'Hawke,' she managed to croak, 'no more.'

His smile deepened, the expression on his face as intent and watchful as that of a cat with a mouse, or a bird, small and afraid, fluttering helplessly under his gaze.

'No more?' he queried. 'But we haven't even started.'

'I said no,' she began, but he wasn't even listening.

'No?' he breathed, eyes agleam. 'Do you think if I wanted you, your silly little refusal would stop me?'

She had no answer to that, no answer at all, and her mind blanked in sudden dread. Did he really mean to force himself on her? For all his fine words, is that what he'd come here for? Rigidly, she held herself erect, away from him. She would fight, fight like a cat, but there was no doubt who would win any physical struggle between them. He would overwhelm her in seconds.

He let her go, abruptly, with a half-smothered oath, his expression etched in ice.

'You're quite safe, but remember, you are

still my wife,' he said.

And she was, legally, at least. But that didn't make her his plaything. Snatching a nightdress from the chest of drawers, she turned her back on him and stalked into the bathroom. Once safely inside, she shut the door with a sharp snap and with one ear constantly cocked towards the bedroom, she hastily rubbed herself dry. Had he gone, she wondered, as she pulled her nightdress over her head.

It was very quiet out in the bedroom, very still, but when she pushed open the door, glancing warily through, Hawke was still very much in evidence, lounging on the bed in his shirtsleeves, shoes kicked off, his tie flung over the nearest chair. Jessica felt her resentment rise, and she clenched her hands at her sides. Husband or not, he needn't think he could make himself at home in her bedroom.

'What are you doing?' she demanded, eyes flashing with furious fire.

'Coming to bed,' he announced, with a quirk of a smile. 'What else?'

His voice was a touch dry, and a warm flush of pink invaded her cheeks at his tone, but she bravely met his eyes.

'Not in here, you're not,' she reiterated sharply. 'Go to your own room.'

'This is my room,' he reminded her grimly.

Stunned, Jessica stared, eyes wide, her voice caught in her throat. Blindly, she lifted a hand to the neck of her nightdress, instinctively clutching it close.

'But I'm sleeping in here,' she finally stuttered.

'Well, don't worry. I don't intend to touch you. Get into bed,' he ordered in exasperation, patting the quilt beside him with barely-concealed impatience. 'You'll be quite safe. I can control myself if you can. But I'm not giving the servants anything to gossip about by sleeping elsewhere again.'

Her colour returned, vividly scarlet. Her thoughts leaped about in her head. How dare he say such a thing, hinting she couldn't resist him? Was he reading her thoughts, her feelings, just like he always had? But she was deathly tired, so there was nothing else for it. Silently, she slipped beneath the quilt, turning her back resolutely on him.

The bed bounced ever so slightly as he got to his feet, making her heart leap erratically into her mouth. Every sense was acutely on edge, her ears straining to hear, attuned to the soft sounds that he made as he moved quietly about the room. Then he rolled into bed beside her.

Stiffly she lay there, scarcelyy daring even to breathe, while the minutes crawled by, each one passing with agonising slowness, but nothing happened, nothing at all.

But resting was easier said than done, at least for her. For what seemed like hours, Jessica stared into the darkness, hopelessly wide-awake. She daren't move, daren't sleep, daren't even roll over since this would bring her face to face with her tormentor.

She could actually feel Hawke's breathing, deep and measured against the back of her neck, and she gritted her teeth in annoyance. He was sleeping soundly like the innocent he certainly wasn't, while she lay rigidly on the edge of the bed. Sighing, she slid farther under the duvet, trying to relax her jumping nerves. There was no earthly point in lying awake all night, worrying. That wouldn't do anyone any good.

But sleep wouldn't be so easy to come by, not tonight, not sharing a bed, lying in the warmth of her husband's body. It would be hours, she sighed, before she would get some sleep. But she yawned and stretched, burying her head on her pillow, and fell immediately fast aslecp!

CHAPTER SIX

Jessica woke the following morning to another quiet day. Outside, not a breath of wind stirred. The morning was still, the pale, early rays of sun touching the leafless trees with light, but there was no easing of the storm raging within her.

Restlessly, she rolled over, but Hawke was gone. Only his image remained to haunt her, the scent of him, the warmth of him. But hot on its heels came another picture, following closely, crushing her heart to breaking point. It was the lovely, compliant image of his first love, Moira Arriannos.

Filled with a terrible desolation, Jessica's shoulders drooped. The baby stirred in his crib, and she rolled out from under the quilt, padding across the velvety carpet to pick him up. Holding him close, she stood at the window, watching as the coming day gradually brought the snowy scene to life. Glen Marr was truly beautiful, but coming back had brought her nothing but heartache.

She should have known it would, she sighed softly, kissing the halo of soft fluff on her son's tiny head. Then harshly, bitterly, she corrected herself. Known? Of course, she'd known. She'd always known. One glimpse of Hawke and she was right back at the beginning again, more in love with him than ever, pushing her self-control to breaking point.

It was never her husband she'd been so frightened of. Commonsense told her that much now. It was her own reactions she hadn't dared trust, her own traitorous feelings if she ever came into contact with him again.

'Come on, young man,' she murmured, turning away from the window at last and settling the baby down for his feed.

There was no earthly use in crying over split milk. It had happened, she had met Hawke again, loved Hawke again, and she just had to deal with it. Nothing had changed, not Hawke, not herself. Leaving Glen Marr was still her only option, as soon as the roads were cleared.

The gong for breakfast sounded almost as soon as she'd finished dressing the baby, and quickly, she found her own clothes for the day. Warm, slender trousers were teamed with a forest-green top in softest cashmere. Then, lifting her son, she carried him down the staircase. But when she finally walked into the dining-room, there was no-one else in sight. Puzzled, she rang the bell, and young Helen hurried into the room.

'Where is everyone?' she enquired. 'Is no-one else having breakfast today?'

'Mrs Arriannos is eating in her room,' Helen replied with a smile, 'and the master went out early. Very early,' she added.

'Oh.'

Jessica shrugged. Pale-faced, she nodded, her features carefully composed. But the words were like a stab in the heart, and she bit her lip at the sharp twist of pain they evoked. Hawke could sleep all night in her bed, for appearance's sake, but he couldn't wait to get away from her in the morning.

'Is that all, Mrs Munro?' the girl queried, breaking into her thoughts.

It took only a moment or two for Jessica to find her voice again, and when she did, its tone was even, unhurried, showing no sign of the tumult raging inside her.

'Not quite,' she managed, the teapot in her hand, paused in pouring herself a piping hot cup of tea. 'Do you think you could look after Gavin for me after breakfast? I'd like to go down to the lodge, to see Lady Margaret, but I think it's too cold outside for him.'

If she'd offered Helen the crown jewels, Jessica doubted if her words would have created a greater stir. The young maid positively glowed, her delighted grin stretching from ear to ear.

'I'd love to,' she breathed, 'and you needn't worry, madam. I've got three little brothers, so I know what to do with babies.'

'I'm sure.'

Jessica nodded, breaking into the youthful chatter with an understanding smile.

'But he'll probably sleep. If you just keep an eye on him while I'm away. I won't be gone long.'

She had to speak to Margaret, to explain. She couldn't run away without saying a word, not a second time, so, half-an-hour later, well wrapped up in a winter coat of scarlet wool, warm boots on her feet to keep out the icy cold, Jessica was picking her way along the snowy drive towards the lodge.

It was a brisk walk with the snow packed hard under her feet, but above her the sky stretched in a limitless arc of palest blue, and there was a sound of birds in the trees to keep her company. By the time she'd covered the half mile or so to Margaret's home, she was quite warm, her cheeks flushed pink with effort. She knocked on the lodge door, her breath hanging misty and white in the clear, windless air.

Margaret herself came to the door, her features creasing into an instant smile the moment she saw her daughter-in-law on the step.

'My dear, what a lovely surprise,' she said in welcome.

Jessica slipped off her boots in the porch, and followed Margaret through to the small living-room. It was warm and very comfortable, with a roaring fire in the hearth.

'Robert is still resting,' Margaret informed her softly. 'Rufus brought the doctor to see him this morning.'

Jessica hid a guilty start. So it wasn't for any

secret, nefarious purposes Hawke had left her so early, but to bring the doctor up from the village to see his father.

'And what did the doctor say?' she asked quickly.

'Oh, he says Robert will be fine, as long as he takes things carefully.'

She left to make some coffee, and Jessica exhaled a slow, shaky breath. Was this really the moment to break bad news, to confirm she was leaving, taking the baby with her? It seemed so cold, so heartless, somehow. Briefly, she tried to resist the idea, but she'd seen for herself the kind of woman Hawke wanted, and it wasn't a woman like her. It was a woman like Moira, soft, biddable, compliant. So how could she stay? It was an intolerable situation, one she would never be able to live with.

Margaret returned, carrying a loaded tray which she slid on to the coffee table, smiling. Jessica accepted a cup, sipping appreciatively at the steaming coffee.

'And how's my precious grandson?' Margaret enquired.

Taken off-guard, Jessica wasn't quite sure what to say. Had Margaret guessed why she was here?

'He's fine,' she answered carefully, then slowly, she raised dark eyes to meet her mother-in-law's soft gaze.

'Are you taking him from us?' came the next

quiet query.

Now thoroughly flustered, Jessica's head seemed to miss a beat, and she took a ragged breath, waiting for it to lurch into erratic movement again.

'I don't know,' she managed at last.

It was no use denying the possibility. Margaret knew her too well for that.

'I'll miss you,' the older woman said.

It wasn't quite the reaction Jessica had expected, this sad acceptance, and her eyes shot to Margaret's face. Had Hawke confided in his mother already? It almost seemed so.

'You think I should go?' she forced out.

'I think you should do what's best.'

Miserably, Jessica nodded. Who could argue with that? But how did she know what was best?

'You've heard we have a guest?' she ventured into the silence, the words dragged from her.

Somehow, she had to ask.

'Rufus has mentioned it,' Margaret replied gently.

Jessica compressed trembling lips into a thin, straight line. I bet he has, she thought to herself. He obviously couldn't wait to move Moira into her place. But it hurt badly to think that Margaret, of all people, was so ready to go along with the idea.

'What do you think of her?' she managed to ask finally, her voice little more than a whisper.

'Moira Arriannos, you mean?' Margaret returned with a slight shrug. 'Of course, she was Moira Fraser when I knew her,' she continued mildly, 'the schoolmaster's daughter. She left Glen Marr when she was little more than a girl, intending to better herself, which by all accounts, she seems to have managed rather well.'

Jessica said nothing, but she swallowed hard. If Margaret could be won over so quickly, how could she rely on anyone else at Glen Marr?

'Hawke seems to think a lot of her,' she blurted out.

'They were very close,' Margaret agreed. 'He didn't think of marrying for a long time after she left.'

There was an abrupt silence, as if Margaret had suddenly realised what she'd said, and she gave an embarrassed laugh.

'My dear, I didn't mean . . .' she began, but it was too late to take the words back and Jessica stiffened, her eyes dark, her features paper-white.

'That Hawke doesn't love me? Has never loved me?' she breathed.

Abruptly, it all made a horrible kind of sense. When he'd finally realised Moira was gone for good, Hawke had turned to her, conveniently, someone young enough to be biddable, to give him an heir.

102

'I'm sure he did love you.'

Margaret's voice broke through the turmoil of her thoughts, but Jessica shook her head, not heeding.

'Are you?' she demanded wildly. 'I'm not. I'm not sure of anything, especially about Hawke.'

Every instinct urged Jessica to escape, to nurse her wounds in private. Margaret just sat, staring, thin hands clutched in her lap. She obviously didn't know what to say next, what to do, and despite her own pain, Jessica couldn't bring herself to walk out.

'Don't worry,' she tried to comfort. 'None of this is your fault, and it's better I know the truth.'

'Is it?'

Margaret didn't sound sure, but try as she might, Jessica couldn't find the right words to convince her. She was too stunned, too hurt herself to think straight.

'Yes,' she repeated dully. 'Now I know what I have to do.'

'Leave,' Margaret sighed, her words scarcely audible.

Jessica's eyes darkened, and her body quivered slightly. She was being brushed off. She could feel it. She was being packed on her way by her wretched husband, leaving her place free for her successor. Stiffly, she glared over at Margaret.

'If that's what you want,' she remarked with

unaccustomed coldness.

'I want Rufus to be happy,' came the quick reply. 'I only hope he knows what he's doing.'

Keeping her feelings hidden was getting harder by the second, so Jessica rose shakily to her feet. She had to get away, now.

'I need to start back,' she insisted, 'for Gavin's feed.'

Margaret didn't try to keep her. She waved goodbye from the doorstep, and Jessica tried to smile back, but with every step along the drive, her hackles rose. Like a snowball accumulating in size as it rolled along, her resentment grew and grew, and by the time she got back to the house, she was positively seething. It was sheer bad luck that the first person she should run into was the sauntering figure of the hapless Moira Arriannos.

The poor woman never knew what hit her. One minute she was making her way to the drawing-room, her eyes resting reflectively on the Jacobean wall panelling. The next, she was in the middle of a storm of truly monumental proportions.

'Hello,' Jessica began, trying at first to be polite. 'It's beautiful, isn't it, the wall panelling?'

'Do you think so?'

Moira sounded far from convinced as she seated herself on the settee nearest to the fire.

'No,' she added, 'I think I'll have it removed, taken out. Then I can have a nice flock wallpaper, in gold, I think, with regency stripes.'

For a moment, Jessica was robbed entirely of the power of speech. The thought of the gleaming panels, rich in history, replaced by some tasteless wallpaper in gold flock clogged her breath solidly in her throat. Carefully, she checked on the baby still sleeping peacefully in his crib, before she deigned to find words to reply.

'Really?' she breathed, her voice deceptively soft, and she waved a hand upwards, towards the centuries-old ceiling beams. 'And what will you do with the beams?' she demanded. 'Have them covered in, with a nice modern, dropped ceiling, no doubt?'

Any person who truly knew Jessica would have recognised the warning signs at once. Even someone who didn't might have hesitated for a second in front of the slight, rigid figure. But Moira wasn't exactly known for her sensitivity, especially where other people's feelings were concerned, and she carried on without a pause.

'What a good idea,' she purred. 'I'll get it done just as soon as I've moved in.'

Without the slightest idea of the effect she was having, Moira chattered on, her bubbling remarks unwittingly adding fuel to the fire already raging in Jessica's heart. Her small chin went up, her hands clenching into tight little fists at her sides. Moving in, did the woman say? Into her house? Had it got that far already? Well, she had something to say about that!

'Who said you were moving in?' she demanded acidly.

Moira turned large eyes towards her, her face puzzled, a picture of childlike confusion.

'Hawke said . . .' she began.

The mere sound of her husband's name on the woman's lips finally proved Jessica's total undoing, and all her pent-up resentment exploded abruptly into speech.

'Did he indeed?' she exclaimed. 'Well, you can't believe everything Hawke says, I'm afraid.'

'But it's his house.'

'And mine, and I'd rather you left it, now.'

Jessica's words surprised even her, but once they were uttered, she meant every one. Her tone couldn't have been more definite, more inflexible, yet Moira still didn't appear to understand. She stared back, refusing to accept, her lips pursed like those of a spoiled, defiant child.

'But Hawke said . . .' she repeated sulkily. 'He said I could . . .'

'Well, I'm saying you can't.'

If she'd struck the woman on her lovely face, Moira couldn't have looked more shocked. Her mouth fell open, and just for a second, her air of childish certainty slipped.

'But he said you wouldn't mind,' she

whined. 'He said you were leaving. He promised . . .'

Once again, the silvery voice had said just the wrong thing, and any vestige of commonsense still urging caution in Jessica's mind deserted her abruptly. Like a mettlesome filly completely out of control, she charged onward regardless.

'Well, I'm not,' she stated sharply, 'but you are. So please go and pack. I'll arrange for you to be taken over to the holiday lodges. There's bound to be one vacant after the storm, and you'll be well looked after there.'

Swiftly, she turned her back, tugging at the bell-pull to summon Helen to the room.

'Where's William?' she asked as soon as the girl arrived, enquiring after the elderly gardener-cum-handyman who lived over the stables.

When she was told he was in the kitchen, eating his lunch, she gave firm orders that he was to take one of the estate's four-wheel drives out of the garage as soon as he'd finished his meal.

'Mrs Arriannos is leaving us,' she added by way of explanation.

Helen was clearly intrigued, shooting Moira a sideways glance, but young as she was, she was far too well trained to say anything.

'Yes, madam,' she nodded, bobbing politely, and she hastily left the room.

Still, Moira hesitated, refusing to move, unable to believe she was actually being

107

dismissed.

'You really mean it?' she hissed, and slowly, Jessica turned to face her, a veiled smile touching her lips.

'I really mean it,' she insisted. 'And I should hurry, if I were you,' she added calmly. 'William won't be long, and you have to pack.'

Moira lifted her head, and with a scornful toss of its tresses, she drew herself upright to her feet.

'Hawke won't like this,' she threatened.

Jessica shrugged, her expression as cool as ice, her own demeanour rock steady. Carefully, she looked Moira up and down.

'Then, my dear Moira, Hawke will just have to put up with it,' she answered flatly.

Without another word, the woman stalked towards the door, and Jessica listened in silence as her footsteps faded into the recesses of the huge house. Shakily, she chewed on her bottom lip as the full weight of what she'd just done filtered into her mind. She had ordered Hawke's precious guest out of the house! Positively ordered her! Had she suddenly gone mad, setting herself up against Hawke like this?

Probably, she reflected gloomily. But, and it was a big but, she couldn't just sit back and let him decide her fate, Gavin's fate as well, not without some kind of fight. Hawke had dragged her back to Glen Marr, now he had to face the consequences.

That thought sustained her through the next half-hour, through supervising Moira personally into the Land-Rover and waving her off, a distinct smile of satisfaction lighting her face. It wasn't until the vehicle disappeared along the frozen, snow-packed drive, that doubts really began to haunt her. Hawke, she knew, was going to be far from pleased.

'I'll face that when the time comes,' she sighed, shrugging the thoughts away.

After all, he'd brought her back. Too bad for him if she'd decided she wanted to stay.

The next hour was taken up with feeding the baby and making him comfortable, then she finished her own lunch with a surprisingly good appetite under the circumstances. Later, back in the drawing-room, relaxing with a book in front of the fire, she took a surprise call from the manager of the holiday lodges confirming Moira's arrival. The telephone lines were obviously working again.

'Mrs Arriannos doesn't seem to be best pleased,' the man confided, 'but we'll do our best to make her comfortable.'

'I'm sure you will,' she reassured him, and she must have sounded convincing enough because his voice was almost cheerful when he rang off.

Resolutely, she took up her book again. She would not give in to her nerves, but the shrill note of the telephone cut into the silence a second time, and she almost jumped out of her skin. It could only be Hawke. But her chin went up. What could he do? This was her house, her home, and she didn't want Moira in it. Quickly, she lifted the receiver, ready to do battle, but it wasn't Hawke's voice that greeted her. It was her sister's.

'Thank goodness I've managed to get hold of you at last,' Fiona blurted out, without much ceremony. 'I was worried to death when I got home and the cottage was empty.'

'Didn't you see the note?'

'Of course I saw the note,' her sister interrupted, 'but it didn't say much, did it? Are you all right?'

It wasn't going to be easy to explain, about the enforced dash back to Glen Marr, the baby's baptism, most of all, about Moira. So Jessica decided to leave all that until later, until she knew what was happening herself. Instead, she spent the time convincing Fiona that everything was fine, and no, she wasn't coming home just yet.

'I want to stay for a time, to see if Hawke and I can work things out, she finished quickly, hoping she sounded more confident about that than she was actually feeling.

'I'm so glad,' Fiona's voice breathed. 'I've had such a guilty conscience lately.'

'Guilty conscience? About what?' Jessica asked, very softly.

Deep down, she had a very good idea. Fiona was her sister, but a sister who'd taken care of

110

her like a mother for years. She wouldn't be able to resist the chance to put things right for her little sister, even if her little sister had very different ideas.

'I told Hawke where to find you,' Fiona admitted slowly, confirming all of Jessica's deepest suspicions.

'You told him about the baby?'

'No, no!' Fiona denied vehemently. 'I left that to you. I just thought he should know where you were. I didn't think he would rush down.'

'That's because you don't know him,' Jessica declared with feeling.

'Well, it seems to have all worked out, doesn't it?'

The voice was small, unsure, and Jessica's heart melted. Fiona loved her. What she'd done, she'd done for the best. Didn't she always?

'Of course,' she concurred, forcing a note of conviction into her tone.

She didn't want Fiona to guess the truth, that things weren't quite as settled as she was trying so hard to make out.

'And Paul?' Fiona queried.

'Gavin,' Jessica corrected softly. 'Hawke wanted the baby called Gavin.'

There was a slight pause before the conversation continued, a pause full of tears Fiona wouldn't allow her sister to hear. Then her voice began speaking again.

'Gavin's a nice name,' she murmured. 'I'm glad Hawke chose it.'

Jessica could almost hear the tremulous smile of relief in her voice.

'So you're staying at Glen Marr?' she added gently.

'I'm staying at Glen Marr,' she confirmed, 'with Hawke and the baby. I've decided I want to try again.'

'Do you, indeed?' a soft voice interrupted, and Jessica turned to find her husband watching her intently from the open door.

His tone didn't exactly inspire confidence, neither did his stony expression, but her reply leaped straight to her lips without a moment's hesitation.

'Yes,' she assured him flatly.

Hawke looked surprised, more than surprised. His eyebrows shot up a whole notch higher, and he shook his head, eyes glittering. Then he spoke slowly and very distinctly.

'We'll have to see about that.'

With a composure that surprised even her, Jessica spoke a last few words to her sister, then with a steady hand, she replaced the receiver. She was not going to be thrown out of her home, be displaced, have her son displaced, and the sooner Hawke realised that, the better it would be for all of them.

'I am staying here,' she stated coolly, 'at Glen Marr, with our son.'

There was no going back, not now, not that

she had any doubts about her decision. The had made up her mind, and without doubt, she could be equally as stubborn as Hawke.

'Just like that?' he demanded.

'Just like that,' she confirmed.

The implication of her words seemed to sink in finally, and Hawke stared down at her. For the second time in as many minutes, she'd rendered her husband speechless. Taken aback, he said not a word, unable to believe the evidence of his own ears, and Jessica smiled, very sweetly, up into his dark face.

'But I don't understand,' he stuttered, and the man clearly didn't.

He had lost his way completely, and he obviously didn't like it. Coldly, he set his mouth into a thin line of displeasure, and he glared down from his great height with hooded, darkened eyes.

'Moira and I have an agreement,' he began, frigidly, saying just the thing to enrage her the most.

The cheek of the man! Thinking he could play fast and loose with her life as he pleased! Jessica gritted her teeth, the angry words flying to her lips.

'Moira has gone,' she informed him stiffly. 'I sent her away myself.'

'You sent her away?' he broke in, his eyes steely, his expression carved in granite. 'And by what right did you do that, may I enquire?'

The tone of his voice was sheer ice, and a

113

tremor coursed along Jessica's spine, chilling her to the bone with sudden dread. Standing there, in the doorway, a harsh frown of displeasure between his dark brows, she had never seen him look so forbidding, or so unapproachable. But then, she sighed, she'd known all along it wouldn't be easy, the path she'd chosen to tread, and she'd come this far. No way would she give up now.

She would fight for her marriage, for the chance to win back her husband, even if he was staring down at her now with baleful, disbelieving eyes. Unflinching, she lifted her gaze, looking him full in his grim, unsmiling face.

'I have the right of being your wife, mistress of Glen Marr,' she reminded him, clearly, calmly, her back ramrod straight. 'This is my home, Gavin's home, and I don't intend to leave it again. So,' she added, 'if that gets in the way of your plans, too bad. You'll have to get used to the idea.'

CHAPTER SEVEN

Jessica held her breath, waiting. The moments seemed to drag on for ever, the silence growing tense and heavy with dread. What on earth would he say? What would he do? Try to pack her off in one of the estate cars as she'd packed Moira earlier that day?

Nervously, she curled trembling fingers into small, anxious fists at her sides, but she didn't drop her gaze. She met his eyes, resolution stiffening her spine. Just let him try, she told herself firmly. Moira wasn't going to push her out of her own home.

'But you've told me so many times it won't work,' Hawke said at last, his tone surprised as he fcigned incredulity. 'We haven't changed, you said. It didn't work beforc you said, so it won't work now.'

The reply was soft, and the truth of it silenced her momentarily, but only momentarily. There was only the briefest of pauses before she plunged on, taking up the gauntlet again.

'Maybe I was wrong,' she admitted slowly.

Now his attention really was caught. One mocking brow rose, and he regarded her intently with compelling blue eyes.

'Wrong?' he queried in disbelief. 'You, my sweet? Surely not.'

He wasn't making it easy for her, but then, she hadn't expected him to.

Shrugging, she tried to find an answer, an answer that made some sense.

'I can make mistakes,' she began.

'Like marrying me,' he broke in at once, his voice harsh, inflexible.

'I didn't say that.'

'Yes, you did. A mistake, you said, that you didn't intend to live with.'

He was quoting her words back at her, and she took a deep, convulsive breath, her heart leaping into erratic double time.

'I was wrong,' she insisted again. 'We were both wrong, but we can try to put things right, for Gavin's sake. Surely he's entitled to both his parents.'

'When I tried to say that, you tossed my words right back at me.'

Her shoulders drooped, and she chewed disconsolately at her bottom lip, trying to stop it from trembling, but it was hard. For the space of a moment, she almost wondered if she would ever be able to reach him.

'I know what I said,' she agreed softly, 'and maybe it wasn't right.'

'My word, you've changed your tune!'

The swift response cut any attempt at conciliation dead in its tracks. It was deeply sarcastic, unbending, and Jessica felt her temper beginning to rise. But this was a time to be cool, in control. The last thing she

116

wanted now was a slanging match. But his gaze was so superior, with a faint, supercilious smile playing about his lips, that it almost killed her to keep the look of composure fixed to her face.

'You brought me back here,' she began, but he cut her words short with a dismissive wave of the hand.

'So what?'

It was the last straw. How dare the man dismiss it as if it meant nothing? Balefully, she glared up at him, cheeks flushed, eyes brilliant with dark fire.

'Really?' she demanded her voice dripping acid. 'Did I imagine you dragged me back here against my will?'

'Maybe.'

'Maybe nothing,' she flashed back. 'And I suppose I imagined Moira's plans for the house as well.'

'Oh, no,' he allowed, 'you didn't imagine that.'

There, he'd admitted it, but there was no pleasure in the victory, nor relief. She'd half-wished, half-hoped for something else, some kind of denial maybe, some explanation she could believe.

'So,' she said, 'you did say she could move into Glen Marr.'

White-faced, she barely whispered the words. They were almost too painful to utter, spearing her heart like the point of a knife.

'I did indeed,' he agreed, 'and why shouldn't I? It is my house.'

Had he really said that? Once again, Jessica felt her temper rising, and this time, she did nothing to stop it.

'What about me?' she exclaimed. 'You dragged me back here when it suited you, and now that it doesn't, you think you can forget it and pack me off again?'

'Pack you off?' he echoed. 'When did I say anything about packing you off?'

'You didn't need to,' she retorted tartly. 'You let Margaret do it for you.'

His brows rose, quirking upwards, but his condescending expression didn't change.

'Mother?' he queried, but Jessica had no time for his glib denials. Hiding behind his mother wasn't worthy of him.

'Yes,' she snapped. 'Margaret couldn't hide it from me, but if you think I'm handing over my home, Gavin's home, to that Arriannos woman, you can think again. I'm not!'

She almost added, so there, but it sounded a mite childish so she managed to bite it back. Hawke hadn't moved, had made no further attempt to defend himself. The absolute picture of self-assurance, he continued to look down at her, his gaze disconcertingly directly.

'Moira?' he queried again. 'But why on earth shouldn't Moira have the house? I don't understand your objections.'

'I know what you're planning,' she spat out,

'but you can forget it right now, because I'm not moving out. I'm staying. It's Moira Arriannos who's got to go.'

She had no idea how long she stood there, her back ramrod stiff. It was probably only seconds, but it felt like hours. Hawke was regarding her closely, too closely for comfort. A tremor slowly traversed the length of her spine, but she wouldn't allow herself to shiver.

Still, Hawke's eyes never left her face, their expression veiled, enigmatic, but he didn't speak, and the silence hung between them, as heavy as lead.

'Well?' she demanded at last, her nerves stretched to breaking point. 'What have you got to say?'

He subjected her to another thorough appraisal, a small frown between his dark brows, then he shrugged his broad shoulders.

'Was I expected to comment?' he asked, a look of surprise flitting over his handsome features. 'I'm sorry, I thought you were doing all the talking.'

His tone was politeness itself, his smile courteous, but he looked so aloof, so distant, that Jessica froze, as still as a statue, her blood chilling in her veins. She didn't know what she'd been expecting, but it certainly wasn't this icy correctness, and for the first time her façade of composure threatened to slip. Was this going to be any good at all, this plan of hers, forcing herself on an unwilling husband?

Could it ever really work?

Her throat felt painfully tight, and hastily, she glanced down, trying to hide the tears starting to gather along her dark lashes. Silently, he came over to lift her chin, so that he could search deep into the misty depths of her eyes.

'Tears?' he murmured, touching one glittering drop with a fingertip. 'Why tears, when you've got everything you want?'

Her immediate instinct was to break free, but she didn't seem to be able to summon the strength. She was tired to the bone, tired of the worry, the subterfuge.

'I haven't got everything I want,' she murmured tremulously.

'But you've got Glen Marr,' he said, finally releasing his grip. 'What more do you want?'

How could she ever tell him, tell him it wasn't the house she wanted? It was him. She could just imagine the superior smile he would cast her way, the mocking glance. It would be too painful, too humiliating. Far better to let him believe she wanted to stay for Gavin's sake.

'I want Gavin's inheritance.'

'But that's never been in doubt,' he insisted. 'So, what is it you really want?'

His tone was soft, deceptively soft, but there was no mistaking the iron in it. He wanted an answer, an answer she couldn't give him.

'I don't know,' was all she could mumble.

'Then maybe you should think about it,' he put in, 'because if, by any chance, you want to stay as my wife, my real wife, then I'll have to tell Moira to buy somewhere else.'

'What?'

'I said, Moira will have to buy somewhere else,' he repeated patiently.

The reply didn't make sense, but then, suddenly, nothing made sense.

'Buy somewhere else?' she whispered. 'But you'd never sell her Glen Marr, would you?'

'I would, if I thought it was the only way to keep you.'

Now the world had truly gone mad. Numb, she glanced up, dark eyes searching blue for some understanding.

'I didn't think you wanted Glen Marr, even for Gavin,' he began again, slowly, carefully enunciating every word. 'You said you wanted a life in the city, where you could study. So, when Moira decided to move back here, I said I'd sell her the house.'

He'd said it again. He'd said he would sell the house, move to the city. Surely her ears were deceiving her.

'You'd sell Glen Marr? For me?' she whispered.

Hawke moved away, crossing the floor to take a seat by the fireside.

'If I had to,' he admitted, 'but it seems you want Glen Marr, after all.'

Jessica stood, still unsure, still numb with

shock, trying to find something sensible to say.

'But I thought you wanted to move Moira in with you,' she blurted out.

'Well,' he returned, 'that was always your trouble, wasn't it? Jumping to conclusions. I only said Moira could have the house. I didn't say a word about me.'

Jessica knew she was gaping like the proverbial village idiot, but she couldn't stop herself.

'But . . . but . . .' she stammered, 'what about Margaret? She said . . .'

'Mother said what I asked her to say,' Hawke broke in smoothly. 'I thought a bit of healthy jealousy was the only way to bring you to your senses, so I asked mother to go along with the pretence.'

Again, Jessica's mind whirled, and she inhaled sharply, taking in a deep, uneven breath. Suddenly, Margaret's implied change of heart made absolute sense.

'You did what?' she demanded incredulously.

'You heard, my sweet, you heard.'

She had heard, but she still found it hard to believe. Trembling, she met his eyes, those glinting, enigmatic, deep blue eyes, and she raised a trembling hand to her throat.

'So it was all a ploy, a deliberate plan to make me jealous of Moira, to keep me here with you.'

Words failed her. She didn't know if she was

angry or glad, or both.

'Well, it worked, didn't it?' he returned serenely. 'It changed your mind faster than anything I could say. I've never seen you so angry.' He grinned. 'You threw the poor woman out, lock, stock and barrel, just for setting her cap at me.'

Now she knew she was mad, and glad. But he sounded so very pleased with himself, she had to say something.

'Maybe,' she tossed out, then she reminded him quickly, 'and you were going to sell Glen Marr, for me. So where does that leave us now?'

'Well, my love, doesn't it leave us together?'

His words were barely discernible, but there was such an agony of hope in his voice that it brought an ache of unshed tears into Jessica's throat. It had taken all this pain, all this pretence, to tell them something they should already know. Hawke wanted her, as much as she wanted him, and nothing else really mattered.

Silently, she looked over at him, seeing his strength, his gentleness, the hope in his eyes, and she smiled. The time had come for the truth.

'Absolutely,' she told him gently, so gently that his breath caught in his throat and he had to swallow hard.

'I love you,' she insisted, 'and I want to be with you, you, my love, wherever you are.

There are no words that can possibly tell you how much.'

He had no words, either, no words at all. He could only stare, unable to even open his mouth. But then, he didn't need to speak. Instead, he rose, taking her into his arms, and he kissed her, very gently, very sweetly, until the room about her disappeared into a golden mist of dreams. Then just as gently, he set her aside.

'But is it enough, this time?' he breathed.

Jessica sighed, and she laid her head on his chest, feeling the tweedy brush of his sports coat under her flushed cheek.

'We can make it enough,' she promised. 'We'll work at it, both of us. When something is this good, this beautiful, I think it's worth fighting for, don't you?'

Hawke took a deep breath, sensing the truth, the honesty in her words, and he drew her towards him again, wrapping his strong arms tightly about her slender form.

'Oh, yes,' he said. 'Though it won't always be easy, my sweet. We can both be stubborn, rash, we both like our own way. But we can try. You'll see, it will be worth it. I'm sure it will be worth it.'

He was smiling now, teasing her very gently, and she relaxed against him, her body draping itself into the warmth of his huge frame.

'It will,' she promised, lifting a hand to brush her fingertips against his cheek, his hair.

'There will be no secrets in future. I'll tell you when I'm unhappy, when I've got problems. I'll even let you deal with some of them for me, sometimes.'

'Good grief!' he exclaimed, his voice startled, and he lifted her away to look down into her face. 'I don't know if I can cope with that.'

'Of course you can.'

She was being deliberately disarming, and he couldn't help but laugh at the beguiling expression on her upturned face. Jessica smiled at the sound of it, vibrating from deep within his massive chest. It had been so long since they'd laughed together, sat together like this, and a lump threatened to block the breath in her throat. How could they have wasted so much time, both obstinately clinging to their pride? They had come so close to losing everything.

But now, that was all behind them, and she curled against him, revelling in the hardness, the strength, the utter gentleness, of his body against hers. She couldn't get close enough, and Hawke loved it. He drew her down, into a chair, on to his knee, savouring the moment, the peace. He knew it wouldn't last, not with Jessica, and as he expected, it didn't.

'Hawke?' she queried.

'What now?' he asked, a wary note creeping into his deep voice.

He could see the faint, speculative

expression creeping over his wife's face, and he knew she was up to something.

'If I'm staying, if I have to keep myself occupied, I was thinking about the lodges. There's not much for children to do over there, especially small children.'

She said no more, she didn't need to. He was well aware of where her mind was taking her.

'And you want to put that right?' he asked in mock alarm.

'If you think I could manage it.'

'I think you could manage anything, if you had a mind to,' he said, giving her a long-suffering glance. 'Just try to remember, it's mainly a sporting complex.'

'But think of the extra success if we could make it into a place for family holidays, too.'

Very slowly, Hawke shook his head, resignation flitting across his face.

'Why not?' He shrugged. 'I suppose I have to thank my lucky stars it's only the house and the lodges you're after! At least you're not leaving me with the business. And,' he added, mischief edging into his voice, 'I'll have the advantage of knowing exactly where you are. I don't feel like spending the rest of my days chasing around the countryside after you!'

'I said I wouldn't leave you again!'

'Just remember that, next time I upset you,' he teased, and he ran a fingertip along the delicate fullness of her lower lip.

She smiled then, softly, happily, into the smooth tweed of his jacket, contentment singing a sweet song through her veins.

'You'll trust me with the lodges?' she asked softly.

She was teasing him now, pushing him gently for a reaction, and Hawke knew exactly what she was playing at.

'I'll trust you with everything,' he returned swiftly.

His eyes were glittering, lit with a thousand flickering flames, telling her clearly what his words did not—that he loved her totally. But she wanted to hear him say it, hear those wonderful words. She wanted to hear his voice, soft with love, whispering them into her ear. She had said them to him. Now it was his turn to say them to her. Eyes downcast, she prompted gravely.

'Are you sure? Do you want me, for myself, or as Gavin's mother?'

'I want you for mine.'

'Really?' she breathed.

'Really,' he insisted. 'I love you, you know I love you. Fiona knew, that's why she rang.'

'You had an odd way of showing it,' she returned with mock-severity. 'You were so angry.'

'I was angry,' he admitted shortly. 'You ran away, sent me divorce papers out of the blue, and when I did find you, I discovered I had a son I knew nothing about. I was angry,' he repeated, 'and hurt. I felt betrayed, rejected, used. But when I saw you again, saw Gavin, I knew at once I had to bring you home, any way I could. I knew I couldn't live without you.'

She couldn't let such an admission pass, not without some comment, but her comment wasn't in words. She took his chin in her hands and brought his face down, right down, to her kiss, and his arms closed in a warm circle around her.

'Why didn't you just tell me?' she demanded, when her lips were finally free again.

'What' he retorted, wide-eyed with disbelief. 'I did try, but with you spitting and snarling at me like an angry cat every time I came near, what chance did I have?'

'You could have tried a bit harder,' she insisted, but he shook his head.

'Would you have listened?' he queried. 'You wanted a divorce, remember. Nothing I said could change your mind about that. So when I saw how jealous you were of Moira, I'm afraid I played on it shamelessly.'

'You were an utter beast, letting me believe you loved her!'

'I never actually said that,' he defended himself.

'You certainly implied it.'

'True,' he allowed with a lofty grin, 'and I thought I had it all worked out, selling the house, moving to the city. I finally thought I'd found the way to win you back. Then you went on and on about Glen Marr, about Gavin's inheritance, and I didn't know if it was me or the house you wanted.'

'I didn't know myself,' she sighed. 'I was so confused, so lost, and so mad when I thought I was losing you to Moira. But I know now,' she added, whispering, 'I want you both. Glen Marr is beautiful and I love it, but it's nothing compared with you. That much I've learned, my love.'

'Thanks to poor Moira.'

He grinned, ruffling her hair with a tender, teasing hand.

'When she came along, it was the answer to all my prayers.'

'I thought she was the answer to all your prayers, too!'

His eyebrows rose disbelievingly, and he threw her a horrified glance.

'Not Moira!' he exclaimed. 'She agrees with everything I say, everything. I can't breathe for her. The woman bores me to death.'

'But,' Jessica said, 'I thought that was the kind of woman you liked, compliant, clinging, never arguing.'

The brows rose even farther, the horror in his expression deepening to almost comical levels.

'Heaven preserve me,' he exclaimed. 'Maybe I thought I did once, but I learned a lesson as well, a real lesson. She was so predictable. Though,' he added slyly, 'I must admit, I let you think the worst. It soon brought you to your senses.'

The remark was smug, insufferable, as it was meant to be. She should have tossed her head, boxed his ears at the very least. But she was too delighted inside to take him seriously. At last, Hawke was saying the things she wanted to hear, and she loved him for it.

'I can see now,' she agreed gravely, dark eyes solemn, 'that you can't do without me. How did I ever doubt it. I might even start calling you Rufus,' she added softly.

'I suppose I could get used to it,' he allowed softly.

'Well, Margaret calls you Rufus, so why shouldn't I?'

'No reason at all,' he agreed. 'I'm sure I won't be able to stop you anyway, so I might as well give in graciously.'

'Rufus it is then,' she insisted. 'It's much softer than Hawke.'

'Anything you say, my sweet.'

Just then the baby cried, making his presence known, as if he wanted to be part of this family scene as well. With a rueful grin, Hawke went over to lift him out of his crib, and Jessica watched, seeing the tender hands holding the tiny form.

'You were right,' she whispered, her eyes alight with love, 'he is just like you, my very own little Rufus.'

'I think I could get used to hearing that,' Hawke said gently.

But this wasn't Hawke. This was Rufus, her beautiful Rufus, and he was smiling at her, his eyes very tender. Carefully, he laid the child back in his crib, sleeping again and content.

'Fiona will be so pleased,' Jessica whispered. 'She always wanted a happy ending.'

'So did Mother and Father, not to mention Alastair and his girls,' he agreed.

'I'd like a daughter one day,' Jessica mused, out of the blue, her dark eyes pensive as she looked down at their sleeping son.

'What? In between running the house and half the lodges, and keeping me and Gavin happy? Will you have time?'

'I'll find the time,' she promised, 'but what about you?'

Tenderly, he pulled her into his arms, where she belonged, where she would always belong, and he held her very close. Their hearts were beating together, in perfect unison.

'Me, my love?' Rufus breathed, his eyes gleaming with soft fire. 'I think it's your best idea yet.'